Connal's Eternal Love
Sweet McKenna Book One

Christine Young

Chapter One

1720
Highlands of Scotland

Connal McKenna paced the tower overlooking the Scottish countryside. Something was wrong tonight, verra wrong. He felt it deep in his soul, the darkest part of his being. It seemed the wind whispered the evil that was close, too close to ignore the feelings in his gut. Running his hands through his thick black hair he decided not to speculate and also not to ignore the sensations that were quickly becoming something he could not disregard.

"What is it?" Brenna, his sister, stood by his side, her hand resting on his back as if attempting to reassure him. "I ken you're not of a mind as we are verging on All Hallows' Eve to enjoy yourself.

"You don't feel it? There are whispers in the air, wicked sounds, and deepest, blackest evil. You are usually more in tune to the wind's undertones than I am," Connal said, turning toward her. "Something in the wind doesn't bode well."

"I ken there is something afoot, but most of it is in your imagination, big brother. Ever since our mother and father died, you have seen shadows where there are none, darkness where there is light. You brood, Connal, and it is not well done of you." She pointed to the hill just a wee bit north. "Bonfires are lit, celebrations are at hand. What will it take to cheer you up?"

"It is not just the death of our parents." He didn't want to acknowledge how Maurina crushed his heart. He felt injured and broken.

He'd thought she was his mate. When he discovered the truth, the pain had been unbearable.

"Maurina then, she has done this to you? She was a *bampot* if I do say so myself."

Perhaps she was an idiot. Not wishing to speak of the woman, his once fiancée, he ignored his sister's question. Sympathy was not needed, as he was better off without her. He had been taken in by her beauty not realizing how self-centered and pretentious she was.

"I'm not wrong about this. There is evil in the air tonight. Something desperate and depraved that will change our lives forever is traveling our way," he paused then looking skyward, "At least it will change my life. I ken it but don't know if the change is for good or evil. When the wind murmurs, I shiver and the sensations deepen."

"I've never known you to be so superstitious or bothered by the undertones soaring with the ever-changing wind," Brenna said, and Connal did not miss the worry in her voice. Yet with an indulgent smile, he said, "You would ken it too, if you weren't constantly stealing glances at the lads in the hall."

This time he was right. They were on the verge of All Hallows' Eve and in the highlands everyone acted strange and the nights were eerie but this was singular. The villagers already set fires on the hilltops, already slaughtered cattle for sacrifice. Usually none of this was done until the night itself. He was not the only one who sensed the evil.

"I'm not mired in fantasy, and this has nothing to do with superstition or the occult. My feelings are based in fact. If you cannot see what is happening right in front of you, you should try opening your eyes, Brenna."

"Just because I've a different opinion does not mean I'm not seeing clearly. My eyes are wide open, Connal McKenna." She turned toward the steps seemingly intent on removing herself. Her back was stiff as she marched away, leaving him to brood even more deeply. She must have changed her mind because she was suddenly beside him again, her hand resting on his back.

A hawk swept by touching Connal on the shoulder then flew

upward. The nearly full moon highlighted the bird's silhouette. A shiver swept down his spine as he watched the sky and listened to the sounds of the earth. This evening every shadow of a noise beckoned to him. He meant to discover the truth, tonight.

The dark silence touched him in ways he couldn't explain to Brenna let alone himself, the world so different now. He believed in the powers of nature, believed that in time people would come to accept who he really was.

"Would you like to go for a run with me?" he asked Brenna, knowing she did not leave the turrets although a few moments ago that had obviously been her intent. "We could swim in the loch when we are finished."

"You want me, a woman, to go for a run with you so close to Samhaim?" She sounded incredulous. "Just as with your fiancée, the good villagers will take exception to who you are if caught. You cannot let yourself become so vulnerable it might cost you your life. I weel nay risk mine."

He almost chuckled but thought better of it when he saw the expression on her beautiful face emphasized by shadows created by the light from the torches. If he didn't understand her so well, he knew she was angry as well as frustrated at him.

"No, I suppose it might not be a good idea. If you were caught..." he let the thought hang unsaid but she finished for him.

"I would be burned as a witch before having a trial, vigilante justice." Her voice shook with raw passion, the emotion emanating from her savage and primal. "Even now more and more people fill our tiny part of Scotland. The chance to roam free and be ourselves is disappearing. The clan is growing restless. Some talk of moving where there is more room."

He was not afraid of these people, those living in the highlands. He didn't feel the need to leave his country. The clan Chattan were different, and they would not be caught, had never been, but he did have to admit the spaces were growing smaller. There was less land to roam free. He understood the need for that freedom.

"We would not have to shift back if we saw anyone. You could stay in your cat form." For some reason, he didn't want to go alone. He tried one more time to convince her. "If someone saw us, I would protect you."

"How? If either of us was captured, we'd be held as a prize to be shown off and would not be able to shift back to human form. Black panthers do not exist naturally in any part of Scotland as you well ken. Don't take any chances."

"I would find a way," he told her but knew in his heart a rescue might not be possible and might result in his capture also. Long ago, the clan Chattan made a pact addressing this very thing. If caught, there would be no rescue from the others. One would need to fend for themselves and find their own way, whatever that might be.

"You should take a couple of the cousins with you and maybe Alistair too. They are all shifters, and you can take care of yourselves, defend each other if the need arises. The four of you together are an impressive force, one to be reckoned with." She hung back from him seemingly afraid his arguments could not be denied much longer.

"Perhaps you are right. I will see what they think. This restlessness is eating at my heart. Pacing the turrets does nothing to ease the feelings in the deepest part of my soul." He leaned against the wall, his forearms on the cold stone, searching the countryside for anything that was tangible or would present danger. He saw nothing, only heard the rumors of the wind.

Moonlight glinted on the nearby lock, the water shimmering and bright. A cold swim might be good for the soul as well as the ache in his heart. He laughed, knowing the water would be frigid and would serve only to numb him for a few hours.

"The lot of you can be as foolish or as daring as you want and," she paused, smiling at him for the first time tonight, "maybe you will work some of this brooding monster from your soul. Perhaps when you return, you will be easier to talk to and live with. You should find a willing woman."

"I'm not brooding nor am I a monster," he grumbled, giving

credence to her words. His gut churned and his mind ached. Good sex would serve to ease him for a little while then all the black feelings would return with a vengeance.

She sighed long and deep, seeming to expect something from him he could not give to her. "You don't have to live with you. You chastised the sweet maid when she spilled a tiny bit of wine on the table this evening. You've spilled more when you were in your cups." She reprimanded him yet the grin on her face told him she was indulging him. "You knew it was an accident. The poor girl tripped on the edge of the rug."

He raked his hands through his hair, the ends flying around his face, coming unleashed from the leather thong he held it with. The dark ends dipped rakishly below his white collar a startling contrast. "I wasn't angry. I just wanted to make sure she understood her behavior wasn't acceptable."

"What does have you brooding more than usual? Really. You need to come to terms with the facts and deal with them logically. Only then will you become a suitable person to live with."

"It's this damn feeling that has settled in my heart. I cannot fight it nor do I understand why the deep weight on my shoulders doesn't go away. It is as if I'm just waiting for something to happen, and I can't do anything about what is coming my way until it presents itself." Years ago, he learned how much he detested surprises. He leaned on the wall once again, his mind wandering, drifting to thoughts of the woman he once believed was his mate. Reflections of Maurina in his head and the words she spoke when she left.

You're a freak of nature.

He recalled the words as well as the inflection in her voice when she spoke them. *Freak of nature.* Because of her knowledge, along with the possibility she would divulge the clans' secrets, she was sent away, far away where she could do no damage to clan Chattan. Her whereabouts was never divulged to him. He supposed that was good. But he also kenned she was sent to the Kinnell stones.

Brenna sighed softly, placing a hand on his back, "You should go now, go run, see if Angus and Fergus will shift and run with you until all these black brooding feelings leave your heart and soul. Perhaps Alistair will be there also. Seems he has the same thoughts as you. He paces and frets, his face grim as he acts as if things plague him over what seems like nothing to me. He cannot find his mate and is questioning now if they exist. I think you will find all three of them in the kitchen flirting with the cook. They are all incorrigible," Brenna laughed, rolling her eyes as if she was thinking of some of their exploits.

Perhaps all that Brenna said was true but a black brooding monster? He was not that bad. Was he? It seemed he did look at everything with a jaundiced and cynical eye. Mayhap he did frown more than he smiled.

Striding down the steps he thought on where they should go. Brenna was right about one thing. They should not run close to any of the villages. There were a few inhabitants who would question seeing three or perhaps four black panthers in this part of the world.

As predicted by his sisters, the three young men were indeed in the kitchen flirting with the cook. When Alistair saw him, he looked up frowning then it seemed Angus and Fergus noticed his arrival as well.

"What are you doing darkening the kitchen?" Angus asked with a chuckle. "Are you going to leave everyone here depressed and moody?"

If that was meant as a joke, the words did not sit well with him. "Wanted to shift, run with the wind. Anyone interested?"

"You would leave the cozy fire at the hearth and a willing woman in your bed to wear yourself out?" Angus asked, laughing, his eyes twinkling with mischief. "Would rather spend the night with a high spirited and eager woman, one who wants to be in my arms as well as my bed."

"Don't have a willing woman, eager or high spirited," Connal muttered, feeling sorry for himself and alone in this world, at least where female companionship was important. "Need to do something tonight. Feel the need deep in my bones. If no one is interested, I'll go by myself."

"Not safe to go alone," Fergus said with a grumble. "Suppose we'll have to leave the warmth of the kitchen and the willing maid," he said as he winked at the lass.

"I've the same need as you," Alistair spoke up, heading to the door. "Where do want to go?"

"I plan on riding north a few miles and away from any hamlets. Looking for privacy and perhaps a way to vanquish the restlessness that is eating at my *verra* soul."

"Dangerous for just the two of you. We'll both go," Angus said, sending his brother a look.

"Then grab a coat and I'll meet you in the stables."

Second thoughts assailed him as he thought about the myriad of things that could go wrong. Two evenings away from All Hallows' Eve and the strange happenings on that night. He inhaled a long deep breath wondering if he should leave his cousins and friend behind, not feeling any danger in his gut, just the bleakness as well as the evil.

He wasn't given the chance of leaving them behind when Alistair arrived seconds behind him with the cousins. Mounted and heading into the darkness accompanied by the murky fluttering shadows, they road at a gallop for a few miles then slowed.

Connal turned his horse down a narrow animal trail, branches hitting him in the face, spider webs clinging to him. He brushed them away with a curse knowing he could be in the warmth of the castle. The trail twisted and turned, going ever deeper into the forest until the only light from the moon was so dim one could barely see his hand in front of his face.

"Think we've gone far enough?" Fergus asked. "Don't see anyone around, don't expect to see anyone but, in this gloom, who would know? One would have to hear or smell them."

"Looks like the best place to me," Angus seemed to agree with his brother. "The only question is can we see to run? It's black as the Earl of Hell's waistcoat."

Connal stopped, sliding off his horse, the other men following. They all disrobed and shifted then ran despite the darkness. Their cat eyes easily adjusting to the blackness surrounding them, they ran. He raced the night and the wind. The big cats were made for speed not endurance so it was not long before they all became winded. Connal sat on his haunches staring at the loch and wondering if the others would follow if he went for a midnight swim. They probably would because none wanted to be left alone this evening as they shared an unbreakable bond.

By the time the men cooled themselves in the frigid loch, a few clouds hung in the sky and a brisk wind picked up. With silent acknowledgement, the men headed for their mounts as well as their clothing. Connal knew the edginess had not vanished, but the night didn't seem quite so bleak or desperate. For a timeless moment, the sounds of evil were slowly being replaced by light and goodness.

"Do you feel better now?" Alistair asked laughing. "I don't. Now I'm cold and tired, ready for my bed. We'll be back late enough there will be no willing women about to warm us."

"Well, suppose I feel the same," Connal admitted chuckling, "but at least now I'll be able to sleep."

"Think so?" Fergus asked, lifting one eyebrow. "For a while this evening I did believe the cook would be in my bed, now I'm sure she's found someone else or she's alone for the night too."

"She likes me better," Angus said, "as well you *ken*."

"Perhaps she would have enjoyed both of us," Fergus said, shooting his brother a look, his voice gruff with raw passion. "We've never shared but there is always a first time."

"Then neither of us would have slept," Angus said, laughing and throwing a shirt at his sibling.

"It's after midnight now. We should get back and still I feel something is about to happen, something that will change my life," Connal muttered, wishing that whatever was about would do it now and end the suspense.

"Then nothing was solved by this midnight romp?" Alistair asked quirking one eyebrow skyward.

Connal was shaking his head while he pulled on his boots. "Nothing so far."

On the trails back, the night seemed to darken even more. Clouds passing across the moon dimmed the already meager light. Everything

Connal felt earlier intensified. When they reached the main road, he pulled up, searching both directions. The sensations no longer felt evil but desperate, fraught with pain. He sensed fear, sheer terror, but it wasn't his.

"Do any of you feel that?" he asked, turning the horse to look away from the McKenna land.

"The wind has shifted," Alistair said, his voice stern. "Perhaps your intuition is better than we thought."

Connal's hand settled on his sword, his heart beating hard. "Be prepared. I sense a fight of some sort. Man or beast, whatever it is, it is coming closer."

He heard the pounding of the hooves, a single horse, but racing down the darkened road, shadows hiding the horse and rider. Suddenly, the silhouetted form raced around the bend in the road, cape and brilliant hair flying behind. Moonlight caught the vibrant strands for a brief moment sending slivers of color to greet his gaze. Connal's heartbeat stopped then slowly began to beat again, the brilliance or the color, shimmering a deep red catching all the meager light until the elements appeared on fire.

Connal's breath caught in his throat, captivated by the site as the woman drew closer. She didn't seem to see them, continuing on her wild ride toward him. Yet to Connal, she seemed remarkably skilled for a woman, vulnerable as well. He only knew of one other woman who could ride that well and that heedlessly without injury. His sister.

When the woman was too close to turn around and race in the opposite direction, "Hold!" Connal raised his sword, moonlight glinting off the steel. Behind him, his men did the same.

She pulled on the reins to stop the stallion's mad dash down the road before she would run into him. The horse reared its front legs rising high, pawing in the air as she clung to him, desperately hanging on.

"No," her whispered word did not escape Connal. The single word sounded and felt like a cry for help.

Yet perhaps he was mistaken. As soon as the young woman controlled the horse, she dashed through the woods away from them. A moment of breathless silence followed before Connal regained his wits, pushing the cobwebs from his brain.

"Stay here and wait for me," he ordered then followed the woman into the trees, hell bent on catching up with her. He suddenly felt alive and whole, all instincts driving him forward to claim the prize that had suddenly appeared in front of him.

He couldn't see or hear her. Pulling to a stop he listened and the silence was foreboding, unnerving. The wind's murmurs no longer sounded evil to him, just fearful. She must have done the same. With nothing to lose, he would wait for her to make her move and when she did, he would have her and discover what caused her frantic and wild race this evening. He would ascertain what motivated her to put herself in such danger.

It did not take long. A few minutes later he heard the swish of movement through the bushes. He smiled; his keen hearing would pay off. She must not realize it, but she was slowly moving toward him. When she was close, he spurred his horse, capturing the reins of hers before she could flee again.

"You are mine now." And he understood his words were true despite the fact she would gainsay him at every turn. His heart beat stronger suddenly and his mind cleared.

"No!" This time her cry was of alarm and horror. "Leave me alone." She tried to push his hand away, swatting at him but to no avail. "I *weel nay* go back."

"I won't hurt you, lass," he said as her fist hit his jaw. Then needing to laugh, "I suppose I didn't see that coming."

"I've heard that before," she grit out, still pushing at his hands, struggling away from him. "You've no right."

"Which part? I won't hurt you or I didn't see it coming."

"Let me go." She jerked on the reins to no avail.

"Stop it." He tried to grab her around the waist to lift her onto his horse, hoping to control her struggles and subdue her in the process yet he realized that would not be an easy feat.

"Never," she said, still hitting at him, her fingernails raking across his face, drawing rivulets of blood. This time she pushed so hard, she fell from her horse.

For a moment, she lay stunned on the ground, gasping for air. That tiny second gave him time to dismount and reach for her. He held her now, once again her arms and legs flying through the air, her efforts directed at him. He wanted to shake some sense into her and tell her she didn't need to fight him. He meant her no harm, but he also understood she wouldn't believe him.

He didn't know what to tell her. She needed to stop this foolishness before one of them got hurt. At this moment, he suspected it would be him who took the brunt of her blows.

"Let me go. You've no right." Her words were short and pained. She was very nearly breathless, exhausted by her desperate thrashing.

The pounding on his chest weakened her until she fell limp in his arms, her head resting against his chest. He heard the long raspy attempts for air, felt the rapid beat of her heart against him. In her gasp for air, a sob rumbled forth. A moment of sympathy or perhaps it was empathy that filled his soul for this lass.

"Now are you going to stop fighting me?" he asked, even as she pulled back, hitting him in the chest with her head then with one last and very weak punch she quit for the moment.

He didn't trust the slender bliss filled moment of peace. "Blessed hell." He'd had enough of this, would take no more this night. He swung her onto his shoulder before whistling for his horse. Interestingly, her steed came as well, but he wasn't about to put her on the mare. There was no trust involved here. If he let her go, she would run and whatever demons were chasing her would catch her. He prayed not before he did. Another chase tonight was not going to happen if he could help it. Meaning to protect her, he intended to keep her close until he understood who she was and what she was about. Why she fought him so hard.

He returned to the road and to a roar of applause from his friends. It appeared at least for the time being she quit fighting him. "A tiny little slip of a woman almost bested you," Angus laughed, chortling with glee. "I can hardly wait to see what comes of this strange union."

"Tis no union, strange or otherwise." But he suspected there might be more truth to Angus' words than he was willing to admit at this moment. He didn't understand why, but this tiny female intrigued and fascinated him. Perhaps it was just because she fought him so desperately. No other lass had ever dared to fight or disagree with him, the laird. All knew that he was the head of the clan.

"Are those scratch marks on your face?" Alistair asked with a chuckle. "Was she trying to mark you or is it just a coincidence?"

Men marked their mate, not the other way around. "Get off your horse and help me. Be careful." Connal handed the girl over to Alistair then pulled the thong from his hair.

"Be glad to," he said, still laughing and finding this situation Connal was in too amusing to ignore.

When he sat his horse, Alistair placed her in front of him, "Tie her hands for me." He was angry now and in almost any other time, he would have explained his actions, but not tonight. His friends could wonder what had gotten into him.

~ * ~

Wynnie understood she'd just hopped from the boiling pot into the fire. Now she leaned against this man's broad chest, pressed so hard against him she felt each breath, her hands useless. She could not fight. Truth be told, she didn't have the energy to struggle let alone voice another protest. Waiting for an additional moment might be prudent, but she was pretty sure she would not get the chance.

"What's your name?"

His voice rumbled against her back reverberating, pulsing. The sound was low and deep, somehow soothing in this turbulent time. This was a man who was used to getting his way in everything. She closed her eyes, praying the leather tying her hands would come undone, wishing she would have seen these men and gone the other way before it was too late.

Resting against him, she tried to draw some energy into her body but she'd been running for days now, sleeping with one eye open. She had barely eaten, finding a few mushrooms on the ground, digging for wild potatoes. Exhaustion tried to steal inside.

"Mine is Connal, Connal McKenna. You can call me Connal. What's yours?" he repeated the question. He held his breath, as if hoping she would answer and he would hear.

She gasped, startled by his voice. She must have dozed for a second, her lashes heavy. Then in a whisper thin voice, "None of your business."

She felt the masculine lift of his shoulders. "Have it your way but I can guarantee I'll be a lot nicer to you if you answer my questions." He chuckled as if he didn't just claim her as a prisoner, as if this was just another day in his life.

Well it wasn't just another day in her life. He was trying to be nice. How dare he, when she knew he had other motives? All men had motives other than what they presented to a woman.

"Where were you in such a hurry to get to?" His probing question was not going to be answered.

"Not here," she told him begrudgingly.

He laughed and that just didn't sit well with her. She tugged on her bindings until her skin was raw.

"You should stop that. You're hurting yourself." His voice was low and smooth reminding her of warm whiskey.

He sounded concerned but she knew she was imagining the tone of his voice. He was just like all the other men she'd known; self-centered, egotistical and filled with himself as well as the masculine arrogance that seemed to ooze from every pore. He would take what he wanted from her as long as he wanted. Understood she would have no say. He would hurt her just as the others had done.

"You could untie me." She tried to add a sugary tone to her voice but that just wasn't her and the words came out more like a command than a flirtatious request.

"Then you'd be hurting me," he laughed again as if something was funny. "I've scratch marks on my face as well as a bruise on my jaw to prove my claim to that fact."

"You afraid of a mere girl?" she asked before realizing she was challenging him instead of giving him what he wanted, sympathy and her compliance.

"There is nothing mere about you." He tossed back at her.

"You should untie her and see what happens. She might warm your bed if you're nicer. Lately, you seem to be lacking in that quality where women are concerned," Angus said appearing to have a good time at his expense.

"No female wants to be in your bed, not one. You're too gloomy and brooding," Fergus jabbed at him. Then to finish the insult, "And menacing."

"What do you think, little lady? Do you want to be in my bed?" He was playing her, his voice assuming a kind gentle tone. She detested the tenor as well as the meaning.

While she did not find him repulsive as she did other men of his ilk, she didn't want to be forced into any man's bed. Somehow, she didn't think he would force her. "No."

"Then you'd rather I put you in the tower prison? You like mice better than men?" he queried. "I can guarantee you the tower is full of mice."

"No." She cringed against his back and was sure he felt the tension in her arms when he mentioned the rodents. Mice weren't as bad as rats. Then it seemed he read her mind.

"She does speak. I've heard there are also rats in the tower though I haven't seen one myself."

She wasn't going to say anything more. He was baiting her and she fell right into the trap. Without saying much at all, he read her body language, the way she reacted to his words. Tears formed in her eyes. She fought them, fought them with everything she could. Yet the last weeks...

"What's your name, lass? I'd like to start over if you don't mind." He wrapped one of his hands around hers.

She discovered her fingers were numb with the cold and the tightly bound leather stopping the flow of blood. Stifling the groan of pain was impossible. He stroked them, perhaps trying to warm her hands but the blood wasn't cooperating.

Wynnie didn't want to give in to the exhaustion and the horror of the last weeks, but her body had different intentions. She slumped against him, her mind hazy. Yet she still heard the words floating around her and about her, teasing words about mice and beds, men as well.

"I'm worried about the lass," Connal said. "Her hands are freezing. She might even now be falling asleep. We all *ken*, she needs to stay awake. Don't want her succumbing to the cold night air."

"We should be home soon and you can warm her up," Angus said, his words filled with humor.

"If I didn't fear for my life when she is not bound, I might be more amenable to a little coaxing or verbal persuasion in order to see her softer side," Connal said, feeling as if this woman was beginning to touch his heart in some strange way.

"Perhaps she's as feisty in bed as she is on the battlefield," Alistair mused. "Think she could be your mate?"

"Not a chance. I would have felt something, wouldn't I?"

A mate?

"Suppose so. Bed her then and send her on her way. She obviously is running from someone or something," Angus seemed to be encouraging. "If perhaps you protected her, she might be eternally grateful and you will be much more biddable."

"The only way she'd bed me would be to force her," Connal said. "I won't do that or seduce her so she thinks she wants me when she really doesn't. Had enough of that ridiculousness with Maurina. The next woman I take to my bed will understand who I am and will want me for those same reasons."

"Then you might be an old man before you get any sex. There are a lot of willing women in the village. You should try one or two for the duration. It will ease your needs and no one will be calling you morose and brooding," Alistair said seeming to watch him as he gave his opinion.

"We're home," Connal said the obvious as he turned his horse into the stables. "Help me with her." He slit the bindings holding her hands and she started to slip from the horse.

"Catch her," Angus said, rushing to reach her before she hit the stable floor.

She landed with a thud, groaning and opening her eyes. "What happened?"

Connal was beside her, stroking her hair away from her face. "Your hair looks as if it's on fire." He murmured so very intrigued with her. Everything about her fascinated him. "You must have fallen asleep. When I cut the bindings, you fell. Guess they were all that was keeping you on the horse."

She didn't move, just stared at the silver-blue eyes looking back at her as well as the row of even white teeth he was showing her. Her breath caught. She swallowed as he slowly set a strand of hair behind her ear. The touch was gentle, not like the ones she endured at the hands of other men. Even when she was running from him, struggling against his brute strength, he'd been gentle with her. She reached up and touched one of the scratches on his cheek.

"Are you going to walk by yourself or do I need to toss you over my shoulder again?" he asked, his voice deep yet also held a hint of humor. "You do know I won't let you get away from me."

She nodded thinking over his words and while she looked around, his men surrounded her.

"I'll walk." She tried to stand but the coldness seemed to have penetrated every muscle she possessed. He extended his hand. She reached out to accept the offer but groaned instead.

"Are you hurt?"

She was shaking her head, "No, no I don't think so. Just cold and stiff, my feet *dinna* want to work."

"But you can't stand or take my hand." His voice was calm, seemed to calm.

"You're right, of course."

He swept her into his arms, striding through the stable to the castle doors then headed up the steps and more steps and more then it seemed an eternity before he kicked a door open with his foot and set her on the paltry bed in the single room.

The mattress was lumpy. Straw poked out of the seams. She looked up at him and knew horror was painted on her face. Eyeing the open door, she was tempted to flee but understood she would not make it to the door before he caught her again.

"You can't mean to have me sleep here." This was horrible, more than horrible. "Am I a prisoner then? What did I do besides run from you?" *Please dear God don't let him touch me. I could not bear the thought of another man taking me against my will.*

"Yes, yes and yes," he smiled at her. "What is wrong with the bed?"

"It's nasty." Despite her circumstance these last few weeks, she was not used to such places.

"Aw, you must be a princess. Prisoners are not usually that picky. But these are your accommodations."

"No." She stood too quickly, falling back to the bed almost at the same time. "Do I get a blanket or water? Food perhaps." Heat rose to her cheeks as her stomach rumbled in protest.

He stood over her, a small grin on his too handsome face. The smile was almost a smirk yet if she wasn't mistaken, it turned hesitant, almost apologetic. "Perhaps if you tell me your name and answer a few questions I would consider your requests. I wouldn't want to stay here either, but you need to tell me who you are and if I should expect someone to be coming for you."

She looked away then back, her eyes appearing to cross with fear, "Wynnie."

"Well, that wasn't too hard now was it? What is your surname?" He held a strand of her brilliant, red hair in his fingers seemingly mesmerized.

She didn't want him to know her last name or where she was from. He would turn her in if he learned anything. Her father and her intended would be searching for her. A few hours before she met Connal on the road she was sure they picked up the trail. She would die before she would let either of those men lay another hand on her.

The wind changed and she heard things whispered through the branches on the trees then through the tiny window in the room. Animals chattered about the events. Evil seemed to find her and settle deep in her soul. They were coming for her. She knew it as the darkness entered her heart. This place was her only chance of escaping them; this man her only protection.

She moistened her lips, looking at him and trying to plead with her eyes. "I can't." she let out a long whoosh of air.

"And why is that?" He sat down beside her. "You in trouble somewhere?" He bounced on the mattress a few times then adjusted his weight. "This bed is lumpy. There is another choice you know." He flashed a brilliant smile, placing her hand in his large one.

"What's the other choice?" She knew what he was thinking, understood the way a man's mind worked. Understood what his smile meant.

"Why can't you tell me your last name?" He persisted, moving his leg so it touched hers.

Heat welled up inside her, a burning warmth, something she'd never felt before. She shook it off as her imagination and jerked away. "What's the other choice?"

"We've reached a stalemate," he laughed, his grin broadening. "You're a formidable opponent, Wynnie with no last name. Shall we continue this tomorrow?"

"No, I need a blanket and water, a place to..."

"A prisoner who wants comforts of home. How ironic."

"You never told me why I'm your prisoner."

He shrugged standing then walked around the room, stopping at the window. "You have a pleasant view of the lake. I think you will enjoy watching the moonlight glimmer on the water. Except for the mattress there is really nothing wrong with this room."

"It's drafty. I would also request something to cover the opening."

"When you're honest with me, I'll give you whatever you ask for."

She was fuming now, her eyes blazing, irritated with him and his strange behavior. Men were all the same. She could not tell him her last name. "If there is a second choice, I'll take it. It can't be worse than here."

Wynnie couldn't help herself, she squealed then screamed when a mouse ran from beneath the bed.

"What's wrong," He turned, pistol in hand, searching the entrance to the room for the object of her fear.

"No-nothing," Her hand at her throat, she gulped in air, her pulse speeding.

"You always scream at nothing?" His voice held contempt and perhaps a huge amount of annoyance. "If you are going to deal well with me, you need to speak the truth."

"So should you." Unwisely she stood up to him. Her voice shook with the realization while expecting the blow. When it didn't come, "You haven't told me why I'm here. You haven't been straight with me about your intentions." She moved closer to him, pressing herself against him as the mouse poked its head from behind an old ragged chair.

"You're haughty for someone who has no rights or friends. Tells me you are used to getting everything your way."

She pointed in the direction of the creature then, "I'll jump out that window."

"The scream was because of the mouse?" He sounded incredulous even while he wrapped an arm around her and pulled her closer to him.

She shivered, pushing against him although she knew she shouldn't. "The mouse..."

"It won't hurt you. Indeed, I do believe it's more scared of you," He laughed outright, continuing to chuckle as the tiny creature scurried from the room. "So you want to try the second choice. You might not like it any better than this one."

"Does it have mice?" She closed her eyes praying for the strength to endure this nightmare of a man. Who did he think he was?

"Not that I've seen." He was still laughing, running his large hand up and down her arm as if he was trying to warm her and soothe her rattled nerves.

"I'll try it."

"No, make the commitment now. I won't be climbing up these steps again tonight. If you choose the second option, that is where you will sleep."

"Will you tell me something about it then?" He was being straight with her. She didn't want to take him up on that option but she couldn't stay here.

"If you tell me your surname."

"Are we back to that?" she asked, realizing he was like a dog with a bone, and he wasn't going to let go but worry it to death. Well, she could be just as stubborn. "Very well, I'm ready to go and I'd like to try to navigate the steps on my own if it's all right with his highness."

"I'm glad you are understanding my status in the castle." He helped her to stand, and this time she could manage, then he offered his arm. "There are a lot of steps. Just say the word if you'd like me to help you more, I am getting used to holding you in my arms."

"I'm sure I'll do well enough. My feet and hands are no longer numb." She spoke primly, she knew. If he could be king of the castle, she could match him and act the queen.

"Shall we then?" he asked, still grinning, his all-knowing expression infuriating.

Immediate misgiving swept through her. He knew more than he let on, obviously, and she was sure now she might regret this hasty decision and the room he was leading her to more than the first one.

They stepped down two levels then turned right. The door they stopped in front of was huge and foreboding. The meaning of its size implicit to anyone who ever lived in a castle. This was the master's chamber, and this was where he was leading her.

His men spoke of his bedding her, but he told them he wouldn't force her nor would he seduce her to the point where she didn't understand or know her mind. Obviously, he lied. Why else would they enter his bedroom, his domain?

"I see by the look on your face, you understand the choice you made." He ushered her inside. Standing back, his arms crossed in front of him it seemed he waited for something.

The room was warm and a fire crackled in the fireplace. Candles lit the chamber, casting shadows along the floor and the walls. The tapestries hanging from ceiling to floor were thick and told a story of panthers and people with the title clan Chattan woven into the fabric.

Clan of the cats.

She looked at him then, really looked at him, her eyes wide with shock or fear she wasn't sure. Then the bed caught her attention. It was huge, obviously made for him as well as room for a partner.

She understood now how so very far out of her element she was. He was the laird here, and his clan were shifters. Knowing the truth left her with ominous and dark sensations. The rumors abounded about these people; some good, some bad but nothing she'd heard was fact, only speculations.

She supposed she would know soon enough what he expected of her. Defiantly, her arms crossed in front of her as if the small gesture would keep him from touching her. She rubbed them, trying to ward off the sudden chill sweeping through her.

One of the other men talked about his mate. She was shaking her head, backing up. She could not be this man's mate. Still behind her he blocked her way as she collided with his chest.

"Not so sure this is where you want to be. Perhaps I can change your mind though." One hand rested gently yet intimidating on her neck, his thumb rubbing tiny circles at the base seeming to warm her from the inside out. His other hand was on her waist.

She was sure he could feel the rapid beating of her pulse, smell her terror, still there was something about this man that fascinated and intrigued her. Raw power emanated from his muscular frame, yet he wore gentleness in his soul. His broad shoulders and long slim torso intrigued her, left her wanting to discover more of him.

Then she reminded herself. He was a man and he would take what he wanted with no regard to her or her wishes or even her pain.

Her voice shaking, "You said you would not force or seduce anyone into your bed." She challenged, hoping he would stand by his words.

"Thought you were asleep when I said that. Guess you weren't. What else did you hear?" Still he didn't remove his hands from her or stop the gentle stroking that seemed to be heating her from the inside out.

"I don't remember." She saw her saddlebag on his bed. "You knew I would agree to this, knew I would not want to be left in the tower room." Anger threatened to explode within even while the unknown had her trembling so hard she thought her knees would buckle.

The door was closed and locked behind her. He was now sitting on his bed pulling items from the satchel. "I need to know more about you as I've a clan to protect and you willingly tell me nothing, Wynnie. Perhaps you are a spy, an enemy of my people. It's my job to safeguard all of them."

Hand shaking, rushing to him, to the bedside, "Stop. You've no right to go through my things." He would find out the truth, learn her last name. She couldn't risk that but knew her meager strength was no match for his.

He would have his way in this. There was naught she could do to prevent it from happening.

"I would do anything," she blurted before she could possibly understand what the word anything might mean to a man such as Connal McKenna, laird of clan Chattan. But the grin on his face told her she might be in deep and very dark trouble.

~ * ~

Unable to sleep Brenna was sitting by the hearth when the cousins and Alistair entered the room, laughing and talking about Connal and the feisty woman he found quite by accident along the road. Deciding she needed to find out more, at least from these very biased friends, she stood and smoothed her skirts before she walked to where they were sitting.

They already had tankards of ale in hand as well as a plate of bread in front of them. She sat down, pouring herself a glass of mulled wine, smiling warmly at Alistair.

"I see something happened. Was it as dark and as dangerous as

Connal thought it would be?" She tilted her head, flirtatiously understanding that with a smile and a toss of her hair, she could get all of these men, especially Alistair, to spill whatever they were keeping to themselves as well as sworn secrets.

"Ah, he found a pantheress to meet his needs, we've been thinking." Angus said before he tossed back his head and drank long and deep then set the metal cup on the table with a resounding thud.

Alistair stared at her then. She felt a sudden rush of heat sweep through her, his gaze resting on her mouth then dropping to her bosom. For a moment she forgot to breathe. Sensations she'd never known before rippled through her body. What little air she could inhale caught deep in the back of her throat as her heart double-timed. What was this?

"We're hoping he'll come down to breakfast in the morning with a smile on his face instead of the frown we usually see," Fergus added to what his brother was saying. "Probably not going to be able to tame her in one night though. She's a spirited lass."

"Don't like the sound of that. Tame her?" Brenna queried, still curious. Yet, Alistair's gaze was still fixed on her almost as if he'd never seen her before. She smiled at him then tossed her hair over her shoulder flirtatiously. His eyes darkened until they were very nearly black. Butterflies flitted in her stomach.

"Ah, we don't mean anything by that. She is high spirited and she won't fall into his arms easily," Fergus said.

"Connal found his mate?" Brenna's spirits lifted. She decided she would intrude on her brother and this woman just to find out a tiny bit more than the men were willing to share.

"Don't know about that but she's beautiful and secretive," Alistair mused stroking his red beard a few times, his concentration still focused on her. "She marked him in a way. Left a set of four tiny scratch marks on his cheek. He could have let her go but for some reason he chased her down and acted as if she was his prisoner. Strange as that sounds, she did nothing to warrant that kind of treatment."

That didn't sound like her brother. "How so?" She leaned forward intent on discovering more about the incident.

"Tied her up, made her ride in front him."

"Really?" This story was growing more intriguing by the second. "Where are they now?"

"Took her to the tower room, but I'll bet they're now in his bedchamber. Tower's not a place for a lady and a laird who has had his share of bad luck with the women in his life."

"A lady? Do you think they will want food and drink? A bath perhaps?" Brenna stood, heading for the kitchen before hearing the answer. It was, after all, her sisterly duty to find out what was happening with her brother.

In the kitchen and directing two servants, she discovered her brother had ordered a bath, for two. She thought over everything her cousins and Alistair told her. The woman wasn't willing, yet she was now in the master chamber alone with Connal. This was just not like him. She felt a sudden and urgent need to interfere or at least make sure the woman was indeed accepting of her lodging.

Alistair was suddenly behind her, his hands on her waist, stroking her. "You shouldn't interfere, lass. This is bigger than you can imagine." His breath whispered along her neck, sending a wave of flames searing through her body. The touch of his tongue where her blood pulsed sent a wealth of never before felt sensations coursing inside. Good god, but she'd known this man her entire life and never experienced anything like this.

She turned, and with a gasp, confused and curious as well, "What are you doing?"

For a moment, he looked just as baffled as she felt. His voice raw and different, "Believe I'm going to kiss you, lass, that is if you won't scratch my cheek. Make you forget your mission upstairs and perhaps find a mission together, possibly in my chamber."

"Alistair, you're a friend." She chastised him but when his warm lips settled over hers and her fingers touched the softness of his beard. She couldn't help but give in to him as well as what he offered. Tiny sounds rippled from her throat as he deepened the kiss. He kissed her again and again, his tongue stroking inside her mouth. She melted into him, clung to the heat of his body. She wanted more and more. This made no sense to her, no sense at all.

"Perhaps we should take this someplace more private," he repeated and this time he seemed more sincere.

"No." Clearly baffled she backed away, running her tongue along her lips. "You would have me in your bed and beneath you, and just because you *dinna* find your mate when you thought you had." Her breath whooshed in and out in short little pants, her hands clasped tightly beneath her chin. "I can't allow that to happen. I'll only give my virginity to my mate."

He smiled then his teeth gleaming white behind the red of his beard. "Are you afraid of me, lass? What harm could a little fun be? Besides, I suddenly believe there is more between us than friendship. I'd like to pursue the possibilities." His coaxing tempted her beguiled her.

"If you bed me, you should be afraid of Connal." She left then, wondering why the sudden attention Alistair was giving her. He'd never hinted at a kiss before this night, had searched for his mate diligently. She touched her lips with a fingertip, remembering the kiss and the warmth as well as the heat.

She gulped air, her heart in her throat. When she closed her eyes for that one moment, she saw them together naked in his bed. She was his mate.

Chapter Two

"Anything?" Connal looked up, a slow purely masculine smile forming as he studied her intensely. Then he pulled out a silken chemise, caressed it with his fingers and brought it to his face to smell. "Lemons. Where do you come from? Will the contents of this bag tell me more about you than you want me to know?"

"If you hand that over, anything. I'm willing to do anything. You would nay be askin' me to do anything I was nay forced to do before." He watched her as she swallowed hard, understanding this was far more difficult for her than he'd ever imagined.

Yet the more she kept secrets the more he needed to understand, the more compelled he was to discover all her truths. He held the satchel up for her, realizing he wanted her to tell her story. The truth as well as trust was too important to him to let this go. "Anything you want to give me."

She grabbed the bag from his hands then quickly stuffed the items back into the satchel. Her face red with embarrassment, "I don't want to give you anything."

"So be it." He leaned against the headboard of the bed and patting the opposite side, "Perhaps in time you will trust me enough to confide your secrets and perhaps in time you will give me something in return for the roof over your head and the food to feed your belly."

"Am I to be a prisoner in this room?" She found a chair to sit in that was located on the far side of the chamber. Then petulantly, "I've seen no food."

Her ploy, the small act of defiance, made him smile. "Only until I can trust you. How long that is, is up to you." He patted the bed again. Then said pleasantly. "Unlike you, I won't bite or scratch or punch and I will see you fed."

"But I would do it again." She paused a few seconds then with a huge breath and indignantly she said, "I didn't bite you."

She was sitting straight and stiff, her hands on the bag visibly quivering. Lord but he would give just about anything to see what she hid from him but then once more he reminded himself he wanted to hear it from her lips. Only then could he trust her. He would never earn her trust by forcing her to his will.

So intent on answers the knock on the door startled him even though he ordered a bath for her then for him. "Come in."

He was surprised once more when his sister entered behind the servants with the hot water. She would meddle. Would believe it was her right to do so. "What are you doing here?"

"Came to meet our guest. We do have other rooms, you know." Brenna looked at him a frown of disapproval marring her lovely face.

"Not that she can stay in." Connal knew his voice was harsh, needing to press home to his sister none of this was her business and she was to keep her opinions to herself. He would deal with Wynnie the way he saw fit even if his sister disapproved. Where Wynnie was concerned, he would do this his way.

"I see." She smiled walking to Wynnie and holding out her hand. Then shooting him a black look, "I'm Brenna, Connal's sister. If you need anything, make sure you let him know. I'll be happy to get it for you if it's within my power."

"I'd like that room you're talking about." Wynnie said so softly spoken Connal had to lean forward to hear her. For some reason he couldn't fathom, he didn't want her out of his sight. He would not give in on this.

Brenna looked to her brother, the scowl on his face, all-consuming. "That's up to the laird. Do you need clothing? I've food and drink on the way. What did you say your name was?"

"Wynnie..."

"Nice name." Brenna strode to a corner of the room then directing her attention toward her brother. "Help me with this."

He did her bidding, lifting the privacy screen and setting it between the room and the tub. His anger seemed to boil over. "You know, little sister, that it will take more than a screen to stop me from doing what I want."

"You mean watching her bathe. Thought you had more respect for women than that, dear brother." She touched her lips before looking at him. "What has happened to you this dark night? You go for a run and return a different man."

It was a guilty look she slanted him and Connal wondered who kissed her. When he got the opportunity, he'd have to sit down with his little sister and discover that truth, the fact she meant to keep from him. She opened the door for the servants bringing food and drink.

"I never intended to watch," he muttered, wishing his sister would leave as he would have when Wynnie bathed but now that he thought on it he wasn't sure what he was going to do. If he left, she might try to escape but not if he took her clothing to get them washed.

"You would leave her alone?" One eyebrow rose in speculation. "Really? The way you are acting right now? I'm having a difficult time believing that."

So far tonight he'd been the brunt of his cousins and friends jokes and now disproval from his sister. He'd had enough censure for the time being. Striding to the door he opened it, waiting for both his sister and servants to vacate his chamber.

The servants left but Brenna stopped at the door, "Have a nice evening, Wynnie. Tell Connal about yourself he puts all his respect into two things, trust and truth. You won't go wrong and you won't remain a prisoner. If you need help, he will give aide to you." With that said she turned to leave, her skirts swirling around her feet.

"Brenna is right, you know. It's what I've been trying to tell you." He didn't wait for her to answer, suspecting Wynnie would remain silent. "The bath is ready for you. I will respect your privacy. Don't wait too long or the water will be cold. If you need any help, just ask." He sat back on the bed and watched as she slowly walked behind the screen.

The silhouette was intriguing, fascinating and so sensual he nearly left the bed to join her. He'd never watched a woman disrobe quite like this. The sight was physical and erotic. His body tightened, inflamed would better define his mood as well as his body when he thought of claiming her, wondering then if she was a virgin, not that it mattered to him.

As the minutes passed, he became too captivated and infatuated with the idea of seeing her naked. He would eventually, but this time he would show her his cat form and see how she responded. If she was anything like Maurina, he would let her go and she could fend for herself. When they first entered the room, her gaze had been fixed on the tapestry. It would be better for her to know from the beginning who he was, who his people were.

No secrets.

He disrobed and quickly changed to his animal form then slowly walked around the screen and sat down in front of her, watching and waiting for a reaction. In the back of his throat, he purred softly.

There was no response and that amazed him. Actually, he wasn't sure what he'd expected from her but not this calm reserve. Her eyes were wide and a dark shade of blue, midnight blue. Her skin was white. Her breast tipped with tight coral buds. She moistened her lips, still gazing into his eyes. He wanted her.

"This is not well done of you, Connal McKenna, and no I'm not a shifter. You told me you would respect my privacy." She tried to cover herself with her hands, but from one second to another he saw every beautiful curve she possessed. He yearned for her in a way he'd never felt before, not even with his once fiancée.

He smiled, thinking of grabbing the huge bath sheet that had been left there and taking it away. If he did that, he'd be deprived of viewing her rising from the water.

Patience was one of his stronger characteristics but he was going to have to call out every iota of it, if he was to best her. Yes, he could wait her out, especially since the water would be taking on a decided chill soon.

Moving closer, his head resting on the lip of the tub, he hoped she would take a chance and touch him. She didn't though. Instead she scooted farther away.

Not wanting to terrify her, he wasn't sure what to do so he backed up and sat on his haunches again. Perhaps he should shift back to his human form so at least they could talk about his revelation, a revelation to his surprise that failed to shock her or even amaze her, neither did it seem to disgust her.

If he did, they would be on equal footing. He grinned and wondered if she could tell what he was thinking. Perhaps she was a witch come to torment him before Samhaim. That, at least, would explain the evil murmurs of the wind, yet he didn't think there was anything evil about this delicate lady. She brandished no black magic.

They would both be naked. He liked that idea but he was sure she would not. Intimidation was not what he meant for tonight. Trust was the issue and at this point in time he wasn't really sure how to go about gaining her confidence and was thinking now that what he did impulsively was wrong and worked against the very thing he sought.

Hell, he was never impulsive. She must have cast a spell on him.

"Are you going to go away before I turn into a prune?" Her soft voice enticed and tempted him, made him want to remain in this spot and see what she would do next.

He shook his head, the only answer he could give in this form. Yet he understood he would have to be equal with her. Backing farther away, he shifted again. Now he was also naked.

"I'd like a bath so if you are not getting out, I'll join you. We could share the water. The tub is big enough." One perfectly shaped eyebrow rose in speculation. Indeed, he put her in a predicament. He handed her one of the towels left for them, holding it out in front of him. Goddess like, she emerged from the water.

He caught a glimpse of her breasts and the sweet curve of her hips as well as her long slim legs before she wrapped herself in the bath sheet, effectively stopping his slow and very male perusal.

Their encounter this evening seemed a coincidence at first,

however now he realized the meeting must have been written in the stars. Fate stepped in and brought her to him. All shifters were meant to find their mate and she was his. There wasn't a doubt in his mind. The problem here was how to convince her of the fact.

He slipped into the water, quickly washing sweat and the fine layer of dust from his body. The soap and water stung when it touched the scratches reminding him she was a woman to be reckoned with. Without thought, he rose, water sluicing from him, turning so she could see him. He paused for a moment before reaching for the towel and drying off.

He wrapped the bath sheet around his waist and joined her on the fur rug in front of the hearth. She was combing her hair. When dry it was wild and free, full of brilliant sun kissed flames, curling sweetly around her face, enhancing every feature.

"I've nothing to wear," she murmured, "Someone took my dress and underclothing. Your sister said she would help me if she could. I take that to mean if you allow it."

"Only because they needed washing. In case you forgot there was blood, my blood, on the bodice of your gown."

She visibly cringed at his words, reaching up to touch his scratches. Her fingers were gentle. "I'm truly sorry. I was frightened, nay terrified of what you would do to me."

"Are you still terrified?"

"Worried and nervous I suppose, but not terrified."

He took the comb from her shaking hands and began running it through her hair. "Your hair is beautiful. It feels like the finest silk and the color matches that of a sunset, no, a deep claret with gold and lighter threads of red running through." He spread the length around her shoulders. "How long does it take to dry?"

"More time than you have," she spoke softly and he wondered what she was thinking now.

Was she still trying to find a way to run, flee from the safety of McKenna hall? "I've patience where you are concerned. Are you tired? Perhaps tomorrow you will tell me something about yourself, other than your name." Now was not the time to regale her with the truth about clan Chattan.

"Truly I would be forever in your debt if you found me something to wear tonight besides this towel." She touched it, making sure it remained secure. "It's damp now and I would most likely take a chill."

"You are already forever in my debt. I've the distinct feeling that my capture of you has saved you from something worse than me. Although I don't like to think of me as someone you would rather avoid." Continuing to run his fingers through the length of her hair, he paused then rose from the floor.

He strode to the armoire and from there he pulled out a white shirt. Tossing it to her, he waited for her to put it on. She closed her eyes, her fingers gripping the fabric as if it were a lifeline.

Moistening her lips, she stared at him but didn't say anything.

"Go ahead, put it on. It's all I have. It won't fit but the shirt will probably cover you to your knees." He grinned, wanting to add that he slept naked, as did everyone who shared his bed, but restrained himself.

She slipped it over her head, letting the towel pool around her ankles. Even with the faint light of the room, the garment showed off her curves more than hid them.

"Where am I going to sleep?" Inadvertently she tugged on the fine Holland linen, her nipples dark circles visible beneath the fabric.

"What are you going to tell me about yourself?" He poured them each a glass of wine before sitting beside her again. She stiffened but didn't move away.

"Not my last name," she hesitated. "You're right. I am running from someone and yes, I believe you are the lesser of two evils."

"Who? I'd like to know. In order to help." He watched her drink the wine then pick at some of the food on the tray. She looked hungry and he wondered how long she'd been running and when was the last time she ate.

She looked at him then down, her fingers tightening around the stem of her glass until her knuckles turned white. After a huge gulp of air, "You won't hand me over to either man? Promise?"

32

"I would not, not if you didn't want them to find you." Unable to resist, he held a strand of hair in his fingers again. *My sweet fire.* "*Mo thine milis.* Can you tell me what has happened between you and these men that is so horrific you put your life in danger without thought?"

"What I've done?" she queried.

"I didn't mean my words to sound accusatory." He was rubbing the strand between his fingers.

She closed her eyes and the slight quiver of her shoulders along with another gulp of air told a story all its own. Wynnie was terrified of someone and most likely in fear for her life.

Her voice a tiny whisper, "I don't really want to tell you. You are nothing to me and would judge my actions. Men always do." Clearly disturbed she set aside the food she'd been eating.

"I can't promise not to judge but I can try to understand." He leaned against the hearth, wrapping an arm around her and drawing her close to him only to find her shuddering before pushing away. He let her go, wondering. Then she turned to him, courageously, he thought, "A few years ago I met a woman, a very pretty woman who stole my heart. And for a time, I thought she was my mate. If I'd had certain facts at my disposal the first time we made love, I would have known the truth."

"So she wasn't?"

"No, you are." He expected her to deny the fact but she didn't. She seemed to be content with listening to his story. "You're not shocked? I thought you would be, at the very least, tell me I was crazy or perhaps that there was no such thing."

"You looked at me a certain way and I saw the truth in your eyes. You cannot be sure and truly I don't see how what you say can be true. I'm neither a shifter nor a witch as you mentioned earlier. I cannot cast spells. If I could I would not be in this predicament that I find myself in now."

He laughed, a gritty sound, harsh in the back of his throat. "You have cast a spell over me whether you *ken* the fact or not. I'm infatuated with you. If you'd allow it, I would take you to my bed this very instant and claim you."

"Why would I cast a spell such as that? I don't want you or any man. Men only hurt women." Her hands were folded in her lap, her eyes downcast for a moment before looking back to him, a challenge perhaps.

He waved a hand in the air, dismissing her questions while at the same time wondering what prompted her comment. In any case he didn't have a logical answer for her. "Needless to say, we'll discover the real truth sooner than later. I know I want you and I don't think you'll refuse me when the time is right."

"Not tonight though?" she asked, turning toward him, her eyes wide, midnight blue pools of incredible passion just waiting for him. "Because you need answers."

"Only because it's too soon. We are just getting to know each other. So, tell me, why do you run from two men and who are they?"

She looked away, plucking at his shirt then with a huge sigh. "When I was fourteen my father started giving me to men for money. My intended was one of those men. In fact, he was the first." She was talking quickly, her words coming out in a mindless scatter that was hard to follow. "The men paid my father to have me anyway they pleased. From that moment on, I tried to stay away from the house. I would slip into the woods and hide. There was a woman, an elderly woman, who would shelter me and she showed me a cave where they never found me. But I wasn't always successful in avoiding them."

His gut churned at her words, fists clenching. "Yet you stayed with your father, remained in his home and allowed that to happen."

Tears were falling from her eyes, sobs wracking her slender body as her story began to meld together into a horrific scenario of lust and greed. Then her shoulders lifted. Her chin tilted up in a small moment of defiance. "Where would I go? Over the years, I saved money, kept the coins hidden until I felt the confidence I needed to leave. Remember, I was only fourteen when all this started."

"When was it you left?" He tried to warm the chill that seemed to encompass her, rubbing his hands up then down her arms even while she tried to distance herself from him.

"A few months ago. Then I ran out of money. I've been sleeping in the forest and eating whatever I could find that was edible. This time of year, there is not much to be found."

"I don't judge you, lass. The judgment is on the men who abused you and your father who sold you." Moisture filled his eyes as she finished her story. All he could do was pray that he would be able to keep her safe and, in the process, change her opinions about men in general, specifically himself.

~ * ~

Wynnie didn't understand why but she was suddenly breaking down and speaking in a rush. Her fear of him had vanished sometime in the last few hours. He would never want her for his mate now that he knew about her past life. She wasn't a virgin and men of his ilk wanted innocent, untried women to marry. They needed to be their first as well as their last. She didn't understand when he spoke of her being his mate. It was just something else about men that confused and terrified her.

"So, you see. I can't possibly be your mate." She was plucking at the shirt again, wishing it fell past her knees. Her toes were cold. While she still sat, the length didn't matter but as soon as she stood, he would see her legs and probably all of the rest of her. She reminded herself he'd already seen all of her naked. All that and he didn't force her.

Not yet.

"No," he spoke slowly. "I don't see anything of the sort." He touched a finger to her cheek, absorbing the salty tears onto his flesh. "No matter what has happened to you, you are still my soul mate."

"Now you're just being kind and perhaps foolish as well." She stood then tugging at the fabric of his shirt, "I'd like to go to bed now."

"Not until you finish eating." He reached for her hand but she sidestepped him. "I don't mind sleeping on that large chair over there if you lend me a blanket and perhaps a pillow if you're feeling generous. I will be comfortable there, more comfortable than sleeping on the ground which has been my bed for many weeks."

His brows furrowed together and she wasn't sure why. "You

should eat. You will waste away to nothing."

"I'm no longer hungry. The food seems to turn to dust in my mouth and my belly seems all a flutter."

"You can wash it down with more wine."

"I don't want to drink too much." No, she needed her wits about her. This man had the ability to wheedle the truth from her when she didn't want to speak it.

"Very well, sleep it is." He walked to the bed, pulling back the covers. "This should do just fine, much more comfortable than the chair."

She remained in one place, her breath catching in her throat. "I won't take your bed and I won't sleep with you tonight. In any case, you don't want me."

"I never said that. Rest assured I want you more than each breath I take. Every second I look at you seems an eternity before you will allow me to claim what is rightfully mine."

She gasped then, startled by his comment and began shaking her head. "I'm not a virgin."

"*Dinna fash* yourself. That fact matters not to me except that I wish I could have met you before all those bad things in your life happened to you. Go to bed now and don't fear me. I will never hurt you."

"You cannot promise that."

"I've things still to do. Perhaps when I return, I'll join you, perhaps I'll take the chair. Funny, you don't look sleepy at all. Would you like me to send Brenna here? The two of you can talk. I believe she has some secrets too. Perhaps she will enlighten you as to who kissed her today and you will in turn pass on the information to me. It is something a big brother needs to know."

She nodded but refused to give in to his wishes. Just because men used her for their selfish lust, she would not give of herself to a man anytime that man snapped his fingers or proclaimed her his mate.

He sighed heavily then, "You're still fighting me and while you've told me a small bit about yourself, I cannot trust you to stay put. There will be a guard at the door. I trust then you will not flee from this room. If the men you spoke of were close on your heels this evening, the best way to avoid them is to remain inside this chamber."

"You don't have to do this, to protect me at the cost of your life." She sat down on the edge of the bed. "Where would I go wearing only your shirt and nothing else?"

"I've no idea, lass, but I take you for a woman of creativity. Left to your own devices, who knows what you might be able to figure out. I was going to have Brenna come upstairs to keep you company as it is still not time to retire but now, well, the two of you putting your minds together, I'm not at all sure a visit would be wise."

She watched him slip on a shirt and his kilt then the rest of his clothing. He was handsome and strong, she thought, as she found herself staring at him. She couldn't help but admire him. What would it hurt if she gave into him and slept with him? What did it matter if she let him pleasure himself with her body? She didn't believe he would hurt her as the others had.

Wynnie realized she trusted Connal McKenna. She told him so much about her that no one else except the men involved knew. Still, she didn't speak of everything, didn't mention the child she lost or the trauma when the men penetrated her. A man wouldn't understand any of those emotions and terror.

The locked door bothered her even though she understood why he would consider it necessary. She tried to believe the guard was to protect her not keep her inside. If she told him her surname, he would not have believed her story. As it was, she was pretty sure he thought she told the truth, but with men one never really knew.

She sat on the hearth then poured herself another glass of wine. He was right, she was hungry but her stomach, over the last few weeks, had shrunk and she couldn't hold very much. She was afraid if she ate all the food he gave her she would be sick.

The huge door creaked open, "Wynnie, it's me, Brenna. Do you want some company?"

"If you can shed some light on your brother, yes." She almost laughed yet didn't dare. While she liked Brenna, she didn't know anything about her and understood she needed to be cautious. Loyalty in the clans was fierce.

Brenna stepped through the door holding a bag. "And if I cannot?" Brenna asked. "I've been sworn to secrecy where my brother is concerned. I've also vowed not to help you escape for any reason you might give. 'Tis dangerous out there as well you ken. Anything can happen in the highlands."

"I don't want to escape. At least for now this is the most pleasant and safe place I've encountered in a very long time. Your brother wants me in his bed, says I'm his mate but I can't be. It's just not possible." She felt as if she was rambling, her words a blur, some things she told Connal some she couldn't remember.

"Why can't you be his mate?" Brenna pulled clothing from the bag, including a long white nightdress, one that would reach from her neck to her toes, possibly farther. She was not as tall as Brenna.

"Are those for me?" Wynnie ran to the bed, going through the items Brenna brought for her. "You are such a dear, thank you. I'm not sure I deserve your kindness. I might be bringing danger and evil to your door. There are bad men who want me."

Brenna sat down, a glass of wine in hand, joining Wynnie. Then, "The evil I believe is here now. It is if you are Wynnie Adair."

The tiny sip of wine spewed from Wynnie's lips. She wiped some of the droplets with the back of her hand. "You know who I am? Connal knows who I am? You've got to help me leave." She was frantic with worry, understanding danger hovered over everyone in the castle.

"I won't do that simply because leaving is not in your best interest. Where would you go? If you *dinna* want the men to find you, the best way to keep that from happening is to remain here, in the laird's chamber. Everyone will believe you are Connal's and that fact alone will keep you safe. No one in the clan will give you up."

"Anywhere my presence wouldn't be detrimental to the McKenna's." Her hand on her chest she tried to breathe and calm her rattled nerves. "They will seek revenge against the clan. My father is powerful."

"The McKenna's thrive and prosper here. That man won't be

allowed to harm you in any way or the clan."

"My father has a lot of power, and he wants me to wed that awful man who has raped me more times than I can count. If we wed, he will continue to do the same as well as give me to his friends for profit and entertainment. I'm naught to them save a plaything. If I ever have baby, a girl, they will do the same to her."

"If you leave here, they will catch you and few in this part of the highlands have as much power as Connal McKenna, laird of clan Chattan. Our people will rally in your defense, particularly if you agree to marry my brother. Will you do that? Become Wynnie McKenna?"

"Marry Connal? I told you I cannot. I'm not a virgin. A man like Connal deserves a wife who has not been brutally used."

"Connal only wants his mate, and he believes he has finally found her," Brenna said. "It's funny." A smile on her face, she paused, "I believe I found my mate tonight also. Connal will not like it at first, but he will have to come to terms with the fact the man is one of his friends, his best and dearest friend."

"You found your mate? Is that the man who Connal says kissed you? I *dinna ken* any of this although I've heard things, rumors."

"With the shifters, your mate follows you through time. When both die, they will find each other in the next rebirth. When Alistair kissed me, I saw our other lives together. I was running with him in the fields, both in our cat form as well as humans."

"You truly believe all that? Connal hasn't kissed me. Just looked at me naked when I was bathing." Wynnie grimaced at the thought until she recalled the way he looked naked while stepping from the tub, water sluicing down his hard, lean body; a god, rising from the water.

"He promised me he would not watch you," Brenna muttered, holding up a gown made from the McKenna clan tartan. "So much for promises and big brothers. They will do what they want when they want. Now, would you like to put on this dress?"

"I thought to dress in that nightgown and go to sleep soon." Wynnie tried to figure out Brenna's expression. "It's been a long day coupled with several long weeks and I'm exhausted."

"I'm afraid that would not be wise, at least not until after the wedding ceremony. I was not joking. You need to wed now, tonight, before your father can lay claim to you and drag you from here."

"Wedding?" she squeaked, alarmed at what Brenna was saying. "In order for Connal to protect you from your father, you must wed him."

"Connal has sent for father Michael. If you are agreeable, the two of you will wed in about a half hour. It is the only way to keep you safe from your fiancé. You do have to agree to this. If you do, I'll help you get dressed and ready. If you don't, Connal will be obligated to hand you over to your father. He will have no choice."

She couldn't breathe, couldn't believe what Brenna was telling her. This was all happening and she wasn't prepared. Marry Connal McKenna? "They will protest. You said my father and Perkins were downstairs." Everything was happening too fast. She couldn't think and knew she shouldn't protest. All that Brenna said was true but wouldn't they also have to consummate the marriage.

"They won't know anything about what is going on in Connal's private chamber until all is finished then the men will allow them to see for themselves that Wynnie, you are no longer under their control." Brenna shook out the dress. "It's lovely isn't it? Our mother wore it on her wedding day. It should fit you fine. The gown is too small for me so it's only right and proper that the dress goes to my brother's wife."

"Why?"

"It is necessary. I suppose for your protection."

Connal strode through the door then, "We've ten minutes to get you clothed properly. The minister will be here then and we will wed whether or not you are wearing only my shirt, although it is fetching on you, or the gown Brenna brought." With that said he turned his attention to putting on his dress plaid and white linen shirt with ruffles down the front, his cravat tied immaculately. Then with a quick nod to Brenna, he left.

"Hurry, we don't have much time," Brenna said, her words sounding frantic and breathless. "Connal and all the rest of them will be here before we can blink. You don't want to be naked when they stride through that door."

True to his word, ten minutes later Connal, the cousins as well as Alistair and the minister strode into the room. He placed Wynnie's hands in his then bending close, "When all the danger has passed, we can have a proper wedding if you would like."

She didn't know what to say or what to expect next. They were standing beside each other, the minister behind them reading from the scriptures. She was terrified. She wasn't really his mate. When he discovered that, he would toss her out. There had been no pretense on her part, but what he would do when the truth was revealed she had no idea. After all, he'd been wrong once before.

Then the minister was announcing their marriage was done and that he could kiss his bride. When his lips found hers, she nearly swooned from the sensations coursing through her. She'd never heated from the inside out, but she'd never really been kissed and so intensely. She never felt so exhilarated even when she was racing her mare across a field. With her hand on his chest, she tried to steady herself, but it seemed all that kept her standing was his hands on her waist.

When he drew away, he grinned, satisfied by the kiss she supposed. She realized she didn't have any visions of the two of them in another life, running in fields or anything else. Disappointment filled her heart and soul. She had been right about the one thing she didn't want to be right about. She wasn't his mate.

When he turned her to face the witnesses, there was applause and cheers. The minister closed the bible with a tiny thud and a grin on his face. "It's about time, Connal McKenna. I was pleased to be the man who married you to this beautiful woman."

"A toast to the newly wedded couple, Wynnie and Connal," Alistair's glass was raised high and he was gazing at Brenna, passion filling his glittering green eyes.

"Perhaps Alistair and Brenna should wed tonight as well," Wynnie spoke softly but it seemed everyone heard and a hush settled around the room.

"What did you say?" Connal sounded surprised as his gaze settled on his sister then Alistair.

Brenna's cheeks burned a bright shade of red her hands on her cheeks as if she tried to cool them. "No, tonight is for the two of you."

"Explain yourself." Connal sounded angry as he spoke to Alistair. "Why would Wynnie say such a thing?"

Alistair looked from one McKenna to the other. "It was earlier this evening that we discovered the truth about ourselves. We are each other's mate. But this is not the time for us. We still have to show ourselves downstairs and convince our guests we know nothing about Wynnie while Connal does his best to consummate the marriage or at least give the impression that he has."

"I apologize for mentioning it," Wynnie said, her voice thin and seemed to be held together by nothing more than a single breath of air, nothing more. "I should not have given anything so important away."

"We will deal with this new revelation later," Brenna said. "All *weel* be fine."

She watched as Connal directed his family from the room. They were alone now and she was fidgeting with her dress, unsure of herself or what she should do.

"What now?"

"If I'm right, we have about five minutes to undress and get into bed together before your father and intended are in this room. My men are permitting this but they will only be here in a moment, just long enough for them to see and understand that you are mine now."

She gasped, startled. She'd thought there would be time to get to know him before she'd be in his bed. Thought there would be more daylight hours between them as well. By the time she caught her breath, his shirt was off, along with his shoes and stockings. Then he was naked and striding toward her.

He must have experience with women's clothing because in a matter of only seconds her dress and underthings were on the floor near his clothing. He swept her into his arms and with only a few strides they landed on the bed and beneath the covers.

"Connal, no, don't do this." She closed her eyes, realizing that once again she would have to go to that place in her mind where she could escape the pain and humiliation.

"Just kiss me lass." He was between her legs, his rod pressing against her belly and she knew what would happen next. He was hard and all male, terrifying.

Tears slipped from her eyes, and she heard his curse, sure the words were directed at her. "You cannot mean to..."

"I cannot," he agreed. "Nor will I. Just kiss me, trust me and everything will be fine. Open your sweet lips for me and I promise you will feel no pain just pleasure."

She heard boots pounding down the hall and shouts.

"Hell. Too soon, way too soon." He reached for his knife. She gasped for air, thinking he was going to kill her. Didn't understand what she saw next.

He pricked two of his fingers. "Now I know there will be no virgin's blood, but I want to make this look real from your father's perspective." He spread the blood on the sheets then his seed. "Pretend, as I'm sure you have every other time that they forced you. Tears are fine. Cry and make sure they believe the pain is real."

"I never cried." She turned her face away. "And the pain is always real."

Her father was first as he burst into the master chamber, Perkins and his guard behind him. "What is the meaning of this?" Connal rose, blood on his rod his seed obvious on the sheets and her legs."

She cringed, curling herself into a silent tiny ball, wishing everyone away.

"She is promised to me," Perkins said with a furious growl. "How dare you take what is mine?"

From behind her Connal's voice boomed with contempt. "You're too late. All the papers are signed and as you can see the marriage has been consummated."

"There should be no blood. She has been well used before this night."

"I suppose I was a little rough. She'll recover." Connal said with an air of indifference.

~ * ~

"What are you going to do about this travesty?" Perkins asked, his voice filled with rage. "They lied to us and it's obvious they were wed only moments before we broke into the room."

"Nothing we can do about it at the moment. No reason we can't find a way to discredit Connal McKenna. When we do, she'll be yours again," Oscar Adair said, feeling the malice for his daughter all the way to his toes. "She will regret this day."

"I don't want to stay in this god forsaken part of Scotland until you figure out what to do," Perkins said. "There are other women who can do my bidding. Wynnie is no longer mine to do with as I please nor do I care."

"She doesn't deserve happiness," Oscar grit out, thinking of his late wife. She abandoned him, leaving him with a daughter he detested. Blessed hell, but he didn't even know if she was his daughter and not some bastard's that his wife dallied with when she should have been in his bed.

When Wynnie turned fourteen, he enjoyed giving her to his friends and watching the pain slash across her eyes. He never expected her to assert herself and run away. She surprised him. It was not well done of her. Somehow, he would get her back.

Alistair escorted the two men downstairs, offered them food and drink, all the while listening to their complaints. The men would not give up, he was sure. Oscar could go to the law, claim he had not given his consent to the marriage. There were myriad ploys the father could enlist to get her back. Connal would have to be watchful. He was concerned now for Brenna. He had no idea what Perkins might try while in this frame of mind. Using Brenna could be his revenge. She should not be alone this evening and he didn't intend to let her out of his sight.

"If you've had your fill, I'll show you to your rooms. I expect you to be gone in the morning," Alistair said, understanding that at some time they would be back. Wynnie was a prize neither would want to give up. Even Perkins though would think a second time when it came to possessing Wynnie. To exact his revenge, he would pick someone else, someone important to Connal.

"Any willing women?" Perkins asked, looking around the hall, which except for Brenna was filled with men.

Alistair followed the direction of Perkins glare. "No, not tonight, not in the hall. The hour is late, I'm sure all have sought their beds. We expect you gone in the morning."

"What about that one?" Perkins nodded toward Brenna, his eyes fixated on her.

Alistair, his gut rolling, strode to her then placed an arm around her, his hand curling around her breast. He grimaced when he heard her tiny gasp of surprise but she seemed to understand and leaned into him, giving his words and actions credence to everyone who watched.

"She is my plaything. Aren't you?" He squeezed her breast and understood from the way her back stiffened he would pay for those words as well as his actions. He would have a great deal of explaining to do. "Come, I'll show you to your rooms." Then to Brenna, "Go on to ours." He nodded to Angus and Fergus before giving her a tiny swat on her backside, something else he would pay for when they were alone. Needing to laugh though, he wanted to see her expression. The confrontation between them was only minutes away and he looked forward to it, enjoyed a feisty woman, one who would let him know how she felt. He wanted no secrets between them.

After showing the two men to rooms in the opposite end of the castle, he strode quickly to his solar, anticipating a night of loving with Brenna. Angus and Fergus stood outside guarding the door.

"She is not in good humor," Angus warned, a smug expression on his face.

"You took advantage of the situation and she was the recipient," Fergus added to Angus' warnings. "But I'm sure in the end you two will find common ground. "Enjoy your evening."

"I believe I can persuade her to my way of thinking," Alistair grinned confidently, knowing he would relish the delicious raw passion that was Brenna McKenna.

He couldn't believe his good fortune in discovering the truth about the two of them. For years he watched her grow up, knew she'd be stunning but never expected her to be his mate. If she were willing, he would claim her tonight. They would wed once the Samhaim was over and the goings on in the castle returned to normal.

When he opened the door, he was barraged with a series of objects: books, candle holders then the pillows. And with each object a new swear word. He laughed, dodging the missals while he slowly made his way to Brenna.

"*Dobber, bawjaws, bassa* you, Alistair!" Then she repeated each word throwing one more item his way. A book nicked his head. He tried to duck as he moved forward, but Brenna had a good aim and she hit him as often as she missed.

Grinning and appreciating the skirmish, he closed in on her. She was breathing hard, her breasts enticing him, still holding a pillow in her hand she hit him then hit him again. He tossed his head back laughing and pulling the weapon from her hands.

"Kiss me, lass. I know you want to." He held her hands behind her back while his mouth descended to meet her sweetly parted lips. It was a short kiss before he said, "I'm sorry I offended you. You can make it up to me." His breath whispered so close to her lips. Then his teeth closed on her bottom lip, tugging slightly as he kissed her, enticed and heated her to a point he hoped she wouldn't refuse more intimate advances.

She squeaked when he slipped his tongue inside her open mouth, traced her teeth and her soft upper lip with his tongue and was delighted when she responded in kind. He swept her into his arms, striding to a huge chair near the fireplace, hoping she would continue willingly.

When he sat down, he kept her on his lap and kissed her again and again. When he stopped, she drew his head closer to her. "You are a *bassa*," she told him but then she kissed him, swept her tongue across his teeth, dueled with his tongue, played and danced. She didn't seem to notice when he slowly began to remove a few layers of her clothing from her body. Thank goodness she was a sensible lass and tonight wore only her dress and chemise.

He explored, finding the warmth of her leg and moving higher until she gasped at the familiarity he claimed. His fingers found intimate soft female flesh, hot and moist for him. His mouth touched upon a veiled nipple.

"Alistair." she breathed in a ragged lungful of air, her pulse beating rapidly at the base of her throat. "We cannot."

"Of course we can. You are my mate. I want to claim you tonight."

"No." She tried to tug her gown up and refasten it, but his questing fingers would not allow such a thing. "You are touching me." She closed her eyes, "You—I never, Alistair." Her voice was a thin wail as he probed her deeply, hoping she would accept him.

"You are hot, and so very wet, your women's flesh is swollen, the petals begging for me, begging for my rod to come inside you. Let me claim you and mark you as mine. Forget everyone else, just live in the moment."

"Not tonight, Alistair. Not before we talk to Connal and receive his blessing. Oh..." I cannot think."

"Don't think, just feel," With his teeth he tugged on her lip again and she moved her legs apart, opening further for his exploration. Her hands slipped through his hair as she arched twisting eagerly against him, giving him more flesh to stroke.

"You are delicious. Wickedly, delicious," he whispered while he struggled from his shirt. He didn't want to take his hands away, didn't want to give her a chance to think.

"Alistair," she sighed into his mouth when he kissed her again.

"Yes..."

"We should nay do this." But this time her protest was weak as her fingers slid into his hair, tugging and pulling him closer.

"But you want to." His kilt dropped from his waist to the floor then her dress followed along with the rest of her clothing. This time he carried her to his bed.

"I do," she said, her voice soft yet he heard the conviction in her words. "Teach me, Alistair."

"Then tonight you are mine and for every night for as long as we live. I vow I will find you again after we are separated by death."

Chapter Three

"I'm sorry, lass. It was the only way I could think of to convince them of your bedding. Thinking the way they do, they understood what I was showing them and that I had consummated our marriage. They have no recourse now but to leave." He did regret the moment, had yearned for something sweet and wonderful between them. At this time, he would have to figure out a way for her to come to terms with this hasty marriage. A marriage she wanted no part of.

Wynnie turned, pulling the bed sheet to cover her breasts. It didn't seem she wanted to talk, just dissolve into the mattress. She was shaking her head now, tears flowing, her back slumped over.

Connal strode to the basin of water then dipping a cloth in it, he walked back to the bed. For a few seconds he watched her, his heart breaking for her. Yet he couldn't allow her to remove herself from the reality of the moment. He tugged on the sheet she was desperately clinging to. "Let me clean you then we can talk."

"There is nothing to talk about and I can clean myself. I've done so many times before. You don't owe me an explanation. I *ken* what this was all about. Though I was humiliated once more by men, always men."

Always men, men humiliated her and hurt her and I just did the same. Unable to control the emotions pulling through him, he shuddered, trying to understand the turmoil that was enveloping him, swamping him. Yet he *kenned* it was nothing like she was feeling.

"Maybe not but I want to explain then ask your forgiveness. This is something I feel you deserve." He handed her the cloth before sitting on the bed with her. "I'm not going away. You are my wife now as well as my mate. We will find a way to make this life a good one."

"I don't want to be naked in front of you." Her words were clipped, her voice weak.

"I've already seen all of you." This was something he could not give her, would not bow down to this wish. If he backed away from her now, that action would set the tone for the rest of their lives. He didn't intend to live a celibate life.

"It doesn't mean there has to be a second time," she said as she turned her back to him, once more opening the sheet so she could wash his seed and blood from her legs.

Wynnie was right of course but, he paused thoughtfully, "They will return you know. Those two men won't give up." He needed to find some way to convince her that he wouldn't hurt her. He just didn't have the words.

He cursed then, running his hands through his hair, needing to leave but understanding he would send the wrong message if he vacated the room, leaving them both alone with their thoughts, his still brooding. What he wanted so badly was his, but he could not have her. He felt as if their lives had been ripped apart. He would not be whole again until she accepted him as her husband.

If Perkins and her father had not shown up tonight...

Pacing the room, he went over every possible argument to convince her, yet he understood any words he could think of would not undo what had been done to Wynnie in her past. They both needed to look to their future together and figure out a way to live their lives whole.

Connal sat down on the chair, head in his hands, wondering still how he could fix this mess.

"You can do what men do. I'll be fine." Her voice and words surprised him. "I won't break, at least so far I haven't."

Do what men do?

She was resigned that any sexual encounter would cause pain. He was determined to show her the difference. Yet, so much had happened that tonight just didn't seem right.

"Go to sleep, Wynnie." His voice was guttural and curt yet he couldn't help the barrage of emotions from showing in his tone.

"I don't want to and I *ken* you're upset with me." Her voice was shaking. "I do want to be a good wife. You can have me, do what you will. I won't argue with you or try to stop you from claiming what is rightfully yours."

"You will be a good wife, I *ken* it. This isn't the time though and I couldn't handle the situation if you're eyes crossed and went dim again. I'm sorry for all you've lost and the fears simmering deep inside. In time you will trust me with your body and your pleasure. But not tonight, Wynnie."

He heard her stifled sob and almost gave in to her dishonest wish. If she told the truth, what she wanted was to be left alone and for him to leave and never return. He decided though he was going to sleep in their bed and he was going to hold her through the night, through her tears and nightmares if she had any.

Perhaps that could be a new beginning.

"Can I have the nightgown Brenna brought to me?" she asked, sitting up, her wild hair flying around her shoulders, her eyes wide.

"No." Blessed hell but he needed to run his fingers through the long strands, feel the silken burn touch his soul and make him whole again. It had been so long since he felt complete. The woman who could give that to him, denied him.

Climbing into bed with her, he pulled her close, her back to his chest. She rested her head on his arm and he knew in a short time it would be numb, but he meant to carry through with this.

"Go to sleep," he murmured, wishing her past away. "I won't make love to you but I do intend to hold you until dawn and the morning light filters through the window."

He did close his eyes and he must have slept. When he opened them, the chamber was lighter. He smiled, though, she must trust him at least in her subconscious. Her hand rested on his chest and she was nestled against him, her breast touching upon him.

Perhaps it was just for the warmth.

He smoothed her hair away from her face, her eyes slowly

opening. She didn't appear surprised or shocked that she was in his bed and his arms. "My god you are beautiful. Did you sleep well?"

"I was warm." She smiled at him, moistening her lips with her small tongue. She pushed away sitting up then seemed to realize she was naked beneath the sheets as was he.

Wynnie surprised him, looking at him then herself, lines furrowing across her forehead.

"You didn't put your rod inside me. While I don't understand why, I'm grateful. I also understand you will." She was still smiling, her hand still resting on his chest. "It is something men do, seem to need. Thank you for waiting for me to get used to you."

Connal needed to see inside her head as well as her heart. He would wait as long as she needed. She was slowly giving him glimpses of herself. "Yes, you're right. I will when you trust me to treat you gently and not cause you pain. I promise someday you will know a woman's pleasure."

"You've said that before but it's not possible. Men cause pain. There is no pleasure for a woman." She shrugged, still naked and delightful, her breasts swaying with each tiny movement.

"You are sure of that." He wanted to dissuade her this moment. Inhaling a deep breath of air for strength, he set his hand on her shoulder.

Then, he ran his finger across her collarbone, then lower between her breasts. Looking up he saw the slight crossing of her eyes. "Don't look down and cross your eyes, don't disappear into some distant place where I can't find you. Look at me Wynnie, at my finger and where it is travelling. Tell yourself this is Connal, say my name and remember everything I've told you about myself." His fingertip lingered on the tight bud, which grew harder with his caress then he moved to the other breast.

She gasped at the sensations he knew he created, staring at him, her eyes wide with seeming wonder, disbelief as well.

"Does this hurt?" he asked as he continued the gentle caress. "You must tell me if it does."

"No..." Her voice wavered.

"How does it make you feel?" His fingers journeyed down her leg, her inner thigh to her knee then back up. He felt the quivering of her muscles, knew she would feel a sensual ache between her legs, yearned to caress the tiny nubbin hidden within her feminine folds.

"Hot."

"Anything else?" His voice was soft and he hoped seductive, prayed also she would realize he would never bring harm to her.

"I don't know?" Her voice thinned to a tiny mew. "I'm embarrassed. Wet, I suppose."

"No need to feel embarrassed or ashamed. Your feelings are good, natural. Your first lesson is complete. All the things you've mentioned means I won't hurt you when I come inside you. Now, let's get up and dress then see what our first day as man and wife has in store for us." He was eager to pursue the day and discover more about Wynnie Adair, now a McKenna of clan Chattan.

She sighed softly, her gaze searching his face for something he couldn't define. "Hopefully my father and Perkins will have left the castle. I couldn't bear to see them again."

"One can always hope." He smiled at her, wishing for one more lesson, but deciding time and seduction was on his side in this journey between them. He needed for her to want his touch so much she would beg. Extending his hand to help her from the bed, she accepted and he was pleased.

A few minutes later, he was dressed and it seemed she wanted to linger. "I'll meet you downstairs. Don't take too long. Would you like me to send up Brenna for you to talk to?"

She still wore just her chemise and stockings. He loved the way she looked half naked, her hair wild and curling around her face. She could be his heaven on earth. Inhaling a deep breath, he strode to her, touched her cheek with the back of his hand.

"I'd like to see Brenna. She listens to me and helps me understand." Her voice was soft yet there was a unique tone to it. She was somehow different today, more relaxed if he had to guess.

So tempting, the smile on her face couldn't be resisted. He made a small kiss to her lips, simple and undemanding but her taste was sweet, intoxicating. Waiting for tonight might be his undoing. He thought of all the private spots in the castle where no one would dare interrupt a tryst then tucked them away for future visits.

He strode out the door and up to the tower where he could see the countryside. The day was gloomy, covered in clouds and threatening rain, matching his inner thoughts, yet for the first time in so long there was also hope in his heart. He turned at the sound of footsteps.

Brenna and Alistair walked towards him. One sight of the couple and the expressions on their faces told a tale he didn't want to hear. His fists tightened and he wondered if he'd have to call his best friend out for sleeping with his sister. Alistair new better as did Brenna. She should have waited for her soul mate.

"Good morning," Brenna stepped forward but Alistair reached out a hand to stop her.

"No, Brenna this explanation is up to me." His voice was gruff while he looked from Brenna to him.

She glared at him but stayed quiet, bowing to his wish. Alistair wrapped an arm around her, drawing her close. Then he began, cautiously at first, "Connal, how was your night?"

"Not, it seems, as good as yours." Connal looked at the happy couple then gritted out. "You slept with my sister. That was not well done of you. I should have your head."

"I did and don't regret a moment. We will wed as soon as it's appropriate, but she will sleep with me every night from now on." Alistair braced his feet apart, clearly ready for the blow that should be coming his way.

"I'm not going to hit you although the thought crossed my mind. Seems I've known you all of my life. You've never been dishonorable with my sister until now. Why?" His demand sounded harsh, but he was the laird and she was his family.

"She's my mate. I've marked her, last night to be exact. I would have waited but Perkins was eyeing Brenna as if she was a delicious morsel just waiting to be tasted. I could *nay* allow that."

Connal understood a need to talk this out with his friend without

Christine Young

his sister hearing every word. "Brenna, will you please see to Wynnie.
She's, well, confused I think yet still terrified of me. Perhaps now that
you know things..." He wasn't sure exactly what to say to her. "You have
a woman's understanding of what goes on between a man and a woman
now. Maybe you can ease Wynnie's fears."

"I was willing, Connal. Alistair didn't take anything I didn't want
to give. He isn't lying. He is my mate. We would have slept together
sooner than later." With that said, she turned and picking up her skirts left
the area as if it was on fire.

Connal leaned against the wall, arms crossed in front of him,
waiting for his friend to speak. Myriads of thoughts scattered through his
head overpowering anything rational. His sister ignored him but he was
sure she would see to Wynnie. It wasn't like Brenna to act that way.

Alistair cleared his throat, seeming to look for time and maybe the
right words to approach the subject. "I've watched Brenna grow up. She
always held a unique place in my heart, but I thought it was because she
was your sister. I never believed..." He cleared his throat again, standing
beside him at the wall. "Until she came of age, I never looked at her except
as a little girl then your sister. Last night was different and when I kissed
her, tasted her essence, I knew the truth as did she."

"That's supposed to make me feel better?" Connal asked, one
eyebrow lifted. "I suppose you treated her right and will from this day
forth. That's all a brother can ask. I would have appreciated some time to
adjust to the new situation between the two of you."

"With Perkins here there was no time. You were dealing with
issues too. I pledged my life to her last night when we claimed each other.
As long as I'm alive, I'll give up my own for her."

"I have to accept this." Understanding swept through him, "I
should be pleased it's you and not some man I despise."

"Would you want anyone else for a brother in law?" Alistair
laughed, looking to the stairs as if he needed to follow Brenna. "We are
best friends."

"No, if I was to handpick a husband you would be at the top of my
list as long as I knew you'd given up all your other women for Brenna.

Have you done that? I know the list was long."

"No longer than yours. I have given them all up, but I haven't spoken to them yet. No one else intrigues me. She is the only woman I want to be with for the rest of my life. I understand you must feel the same about Wynnie."

"Yes, but our night was not so pleasant. We've a long ways to go before she will give herself willingly to me. I take it Perkins and Wynnie's father have left the castle."

"You can just see their dust right now." Alistair pointed down the road. "I feel a sigh of relief sweeping through the castle walls."

Connal let out a long slow breath of air. "They will be back and at the moment I've no hopes that Wynnie will be with child by the time they return, looking to steal her away."

"She is your wife and your mate, with child or without should make no difference in the eyes of the law," Alistair said.

"They will say I'm a thief stealing her away and will have righteousness on their side. How do I go about bedding my wife who is terrified of men?" *And with good reason.*

Alistair turned toward him, "Slowly very slowly, one small step at a time and she will eventually give you her heart."

~ * ~

Moisture in her eyes, Wynnie sat on the sofa, staring at the door and remembering the way Connal left. He wasn't angry exactly, just perhaps frustrated and wanting more from her. Brooding might be a good word to describe him. She knew he wanted more of her. She'd offered but he refused because he understood she was terrified.

She didn't know what to do or how to fix the problem.

The door squeaked open. Brenna poked her head around the corner, "Hello? Would you like company? Connal and Alistair sent me away, and Connal made the suggestion you might want to talk."

"I'm not really fit for company but yes, if you can stand the tears and self-pity, I'd love to have someone to speak with." Wynnie didn't know how talking to Brenna could help, but she was eager to try everything.

"I'm a willing listener and I happen to comprehend the cause of those tears and self-pity very well. Connal is a gentle man, big but gentle. He is even loathe to kill flies." Brenna laughed softly seeming to think about her words. "Well, maybe not flies."

Wynnie fiddled with the lace on her gown, one Brenna had given her. She didn't like feeling beholding, but Brenna was sweet and generous. "Connal is not the cause. It's my father, and Perkins too. I told Connal last night he could have me and he told me to stop crossing my eyes."

Brenna laughed softly, "Only my brother would say something like that. Do you cross your eyes when a man kisses you?"

She shrugged wondering about kisses. "Don't know, never been kissed before yesterday, but I do cross my eyes and go to someplace where I can't feel or see anything when..." Wynnie said with a long sigh not wanting to finish. Brenna didn't need to hear her story. "I want to please him but I don't know how. Can you help?"

"I don't know much about lovemaking and pleasing men," Brenna said. "Just what I learned last night."

"We are both ignorant females then." Wynnie turned away, more moisture welling in her eyes and threatening to fall. "I just don't know what to do. If I keep this up, my face will be puffy and eyes swollen. He won't want anything to do with me."

"You will most likely still be beautiful to him."

"Even with red swollen eyes? Perkins says I'm ugly when I look like that, but it kept him away from me sometimes, not the other men though, never anyone else."

"I'm not entirely ignorant," Brenna volunteered. "I slept with Alistair last night. We made love but... I don't think I can give you any advice. It was all so new."

"I understand," Wynnie said, looking down, sure now she would never figure out how to please Connal.

Brenna turned toward her, a smile on her face. "No, listen. I think you should put this in the hands of your mate. He will figure it out for the both of you. Trust him and I'm sure this will all turn out the way you want."

"You make it sound so easy." She was shaking her head, wishing she felt a bit more eager to see Connal again. "It's impossible and now he's so busy with everything. You know he left this morning without me right after he said we should see what the day has in store for us."

"I'm sure you misunderstood. He will be pleased to see you and you cannot deny the fact he married you knowing about your past."

"He just felt obligated and sorry for me," Wynnie said, walking to the window, still feeling sorry for herself when she should be feeling ecstatic that she was no longer on the run from her father.

"A man like my brother would never marry anyone if all he felt for her was obligation or pity. Connal would have found a means to help you in some other way."

"I want to believe you, it's just that..."

"Stop that, we're going downstairs and see what is happening. You'll be surprised to see the smile on Connal's face, but I won't."

She was hesitant but the huge grin on Brenna's face gave her a small measure of hope. Wynnie was nodding her head in agreement even while Brenna stood at the door, waiting for her.

"Let's try the tower first," Brenna said, opening the door for her.

Wynnie waited outside, unsure of where to go. If left alone, she wouldn't know which hallway to go down or what stairs to take. She would find herself lost in no time. Brenna nodded towards the left, which brought them to the stairs leading upwards. She lifted her skirts, taking each step with hesitation.

At the top, Alistair stood next to Connal. They appeared to be deep in conversation and Wynnie started to turn, changing her mind about the prudence of meeting him.

"No, you don't," Brenna said, softly the hint of laughter in her voice. "If you ask me, which of course you haven't, there is no better time than the present to show your trust in him."

Wynnie held back, watching as Brenna walked towards the men, her back straight, confident. She wished she could feel so poised and sure of herself. Wrapping her arms around her waist, she stared as both men slowly turned towards them.

Connal's face lit in a wide grin as did Alistair's, but Wynnie couldn't be sure if Connal was pleased to see her or his sister. Her mind was changed when Connal stepped past his sister, his arms open wide, she assumed for her. To make sure she glanced behind her.

"Wynnie." He embraced her, drawing her close.

He was warm and strong. In his arms she felt protected and safe. She rested her head against his chest hearing his strong, steady heartbeat.

"I've missed you. Did you enjoy your talk with Brenna?" he asked, still holding her with one hand but running his fingers through her hair with the other.

"Think we'll leave the two of you alone," Alistair said, his voice gruff with passion as his gaze remained fixed on Brenna. He extended his arm, Brenna accepting. "Would you like to go somewhere private?"

Brenna nodded, leaning into Alistair. Their relationship seemed to be one of love as well as ease. It appeared to Wynnie they loved each other very much. She turned to Connal, wondering if there would ever be love between them.

He was holding his hand out to her. She stared at him a few seconds then placed her hand in his. Pulling her towards him, he wrapped his arms around her. "Ah, lass, I'm glad to see you came up here. But it must have been Brenna's idea. She knew we were on the parapets when she left us."

Wynnie rested her head on his chest, afraid to meet his gaze then inhaled deeply, hoping the new air in her lungs would fill her with enough courage to proceed. Thoughts of trying to seduce him flitted through her head. Having no idea how to do such a thing, she shoved them aside.

"Yes, Brenna thought you would be here," Wynnie said as she pushed slightly away, looking up and into his eyes which seemed to be filled with raw passion. She gasped and tried to move away but he was too strong, just as Perkins and the other men had been.

Then to her surprise, he let go. "I will never hold you against your will." But there was a deep undercurrent of sorrow in his voice.

"No." She stepped closer. "You are not Perkins. It's just that my reactions come from ghosts of the past, which haunt my days as well as my nights. I would have your help in vanquishing these demons of mine."

"Kiss me." Connal's gentle smile warmed her heart.

"I..."

"'Tis just a kiss, lass," he prompted, his hands behind his back. "I want nothing more from you."

She sucked her bottom lip between her teeth before blurting. "I *dinna ken* how to kiss."

"Certainly..." he stopped, rubbing his chin as if thinking. "No one, not one of the men... Should I kiss you, Wynnie? Would you like that? Then, if you want to kiss me you'll know what to do."

"Brenna told me she liked Alistair's kisses." She hoped Connal would not be put off for what she said and what she didn't know how to do. "Don't most men like to be kissed too?"

"I would laugh because you are so very sweet and gentle and despite your past, you are innocent beyond belief, but you might take offense. Aye, most men loved to be kissed by pretty girls and I'm no different. I also take great delight in kissing pretty girls."

"Father says I'm passable but my breasts are too small. He told me men would enjoy me more if parts of me were larger." Wynnie wasn't sure why she told Connal that, but she was terrified when rage seemed to possess his expression.

"How I feel about you is all that matters. Your father is an idiot, a *bampot* and a horrible man," Connal said in an outburst. "Now let's see about kissing. It's a very good idea you have."

"I've seen people kissing," she said.

"Good then you've some idea as to how it goes."

"Perhaps if I'm to kiss you I could use a footstool." She smiled at him then, thinking she would have to jump up and down to reach him.

He did laugh then, touched her lips with his finger. "I will not make this difficult, and since I'm to kiss you first, well, then I will bend down close to you."

With his hand around her waist, he pulled her closer. She felt his hard body against hers and remembered the way he looked just this morning when he rose naked from their bed. She swallowed, wondering what would come next, but his lips hovered close to hers without touching.

She ran her tongue across her lips and touched his mouth. A startled gasp escaped her. He chuckled softly. "That was a start." Then his lips found hers so very gently she wasn't at all sure he was kissing her. He drew away then and smiled at her.

"Is that all there is?" she asked as he put some distance between them. "I thought there was more."

"You're right, of course. It's your turn now." Once again, he bent close to her, his lips only a fraction from hers, waiting.

Wynnie ran her hands through his hair, enjoying the softness before touching his lips with hers. She touched then pulled back then touched him again. He slid his tongue across the seam and she gasped again, startled by the simple yet mercuric sensations the contact summoned.

"That was good, very good," he told her, taking her arm in his. "Shall we go downstairs and I'll introduce you to some of our people?"

"That's it? I expected something more."

"I enjoyed your kiss very much. Did you want a third kiss? Greedy girl," he laughed seeming pleased with himself. "Perhaps tonight I'll let you kiss me again.

~ * ~

Adair and Perkins stopped at the first inn they came across that morning. They were only a few miles from the McKenna castle. Perkins wanted to stay on McKenna land, but Oscar thought it would be best to wait a few months before returning, lull Wynnie and the laird into a sense of comfort and leave them unsuspecting.

"Wynnie won't be able to stay in the confines of the castle for more than a few days," Perkins argued his case, thinking if they stayed here, they would find her alone and vulnerable sooner than later.

"She has someone to keep her tied up if she tries to leave. I wouldn't put it past Connal McKenna to do just that if she acted foolishly," Oscar said. "I've the strange feeling he'll be the first man she obeys.

"Well, in any case, I'm not all that sure I want used goods." Perkins laughed at himself. "Used by other than those I've hand picked. What if he does get her pregnant?"

Oscar shrugged. "McKenna will fight all the harder to keep her close. What you have to decide is if it's your pride that wants her or if you really do like to have her beneath you and at your whim."

"Both," Perkins said quickly, rubbing his crotch, remembering the way he felt when he forced her and was deep inside her. "I want both. She was always such a willful lass and full of her self worth. She looked down her nose at me too many times, and it was fun to tame her. I need to keep making her pay."

"You've always needed everything." Oscar smiled, "That's why I picked you first."

"We'll do this your way. Go home, figure out what we have on our side and bring the necessary witnesses. We could claim I married Wynnie before she fled."

"I know just the person to forge the proper documents," Oscar said. "This won't be too difficult. Your marriage to Wynnie should prevail, don't you think?"

Chapter Four

Connal wasn't sure where to go from here, his body tense with barely controlled agony. He needed release and there were only a few ways to gain it. Two were not possible at the moment.

He watched Alistair, relaxed and at ease, chatting with Brenna in the hall. His fists clenched. His best friend's relationship with his sister still left him with misgivings, understanding the reasons he claimed her without benefit of marriage but the act still left distaste in his mouth.

With Wynnie by his side, he strode to his sister and his friend. The need still encapsulating him, "Let's takes this outside." He addressed his statement to Alistair who seemed to immediately understand what it was he wanted..

"Fists or steel?" Alistair laughed, seeming to understand what was driving him and the need to hit something.

"Swords first," Connal gritted out, then to Wynnie, "Stay here with Brenna. The two of you can get to know each other better."

Wynnie looked to him, her forehead creased between her eyes then to Brenna. "If Brenna has nothing better to do. I suppose." She seemed to hesitate. "I do have things I would like to ask her."

Brenna reached out to her. "Please sit. You must want something to eat and drink. We will watch them later. They will work out whatever is bothering them then they'll want some solace from us. Our men folk tend to beat themselves to a bloody pulp under the guise of feeling better then they want their woman to tend to and heal their wounds."

Wynnie looked to him again. He tried to smile, "Go on, Brenna is right in all she has said." It seemed once again he was abandoning Wynnie to his sister so she could make things right between them. He ran both hands through his hair, wishing he had some way to make things right with Wynnie. A short talk with his sister would not break down the barrier between them.

But he had no ideas.

In the yard, the two men met, steel meeting steel, ducking and parrying, the pair seemed to enjoy the fight. Clashing steel rang out in the courtyard and with each jarring noise, the grunts of the men were heard as they put all possible effort into their blows.

Seconds ticked by turning into minutes. Sweat dripped into Connal's eyes, his muscles strained with each blow. The metal met above their heads as they pushed to gain supremacy.

The men were equally matched in many ways. Connal was quicker, faster on his feet, but Alistair bested him with brute strength and bulk. They shoved against each other, both men falling back and tossing their swords to the side.

Alistair roared, lunging at him while Connal met him head on, the two men grappling together trying to best the other. Rolling on the ground in the mud and the dirt the grunts seemed to be one with each punch. Somehow Connal slipped from Alistair's grip.

Bent, feet dancing, they circled each other, looking for a weakness. Alistair lashed out and Connal ducked and whirled landing a kick to Alistair's side, eliciting another grunt. Connal guarded his face and upper torso to block the ferocious blows his opponent rained down upon him. He spun and ducked again. Alistair fought, countered the attack, but this time he did not move fast enough. Connal's next punch was so fast and so hard Alistair didn't block the punch. He staggered backwards, blood running from his nose. The crowd that gathered around them yelled and cheered for the two combatants. Alistair roared and bent over attacked Connal around the waist and they fell to the ground again, rolling on the earth as each tried to win.

Then they were both sprawled on their back, laughing. "You didn't have to hit me so hard." Alistair moaned through gritted teeth. "Thought we were friends."

"Seems to me you could have been a wee bit gentler," Connal shot back. "With me and my sister."

"And what good would that have done?" Alistair asked, rising from the ground and extending a hand to help Connal stand. "Neither one of us would feel better. As soon as I see Brenna all sensation will coming rushing back."

"Not sure I feel better anyway," he said, breathing heavily, winded by the conflict with his friend. "Still have to face another night with Wynnie and figure out just how I'm going to ease her mind about me."

"Know only one thing that will make either of us feel better," Alistair said, looking through the crowd.

Connal followed the direction of Alistair's gaze to see Brenna and Wynnie standing on the sidelines watching. Wynnie's eyes were huge pools of dark blue. He didn't have any idea what she was thinking but she appeared horrified. This was not the way he wanted to deal with her.

One small intimacy at a time was prudent. If he terrified her, he would be taking steps backwards in their tenuous relationship. He stood then arms spread wide as his men dumped a bucket of water over his head, intended to wash most of the dirt and sweat from his body before he entered into the main hall.

Trying to catch Wynnie's attention, he smiled at her. The thought that she was afraid for him crossed his mind, but he set the notion aside as being ridiculous. She probably hoped for his demise... no, that would not be wise and he thought of Wynnie as an intelligent woman who would understand he protected her from a worse fate than himself.

He exhaled a long slow breath of air, wishing for a different relationship with her. While he never believed in undying romantic love, he did acknowledge she was his mate for life. He didn't know how to win her over to his way of thinking or his bed though. Alistair told him one sweet kiss at a time, but she barely allowed a touch between them let alone a kiss. What few intimacies they shared had been forced upon them by circumstances. Except for the encounter earlier today on the parapets. She appeared eager to learn.

"All you need do is court her as if she was a virgin. She is in a way," Brenna stood by his side while Alistair seemed to be glowering at her. "Pretend you are just as afraid of touching her as she is of you."

He shook his head, watching as water droplets littered the air around him and Brenna stepped back, grimacing at him. "Don't know how to court a lady. Don't know anything about the gentler side of women. Never was afraid to touch a woman or a girl even when I was younger for that matter. She would never believe it if I tried."

"You didn't court Maurina?" Brenna asked, puzzled by his announcement. "There must have been some hesitancy with the first kiss."

"Don't remember," he muttered. "Doubt it. I *wasnae* her first lover."

"Come." Alistair was by her side, his hand resting possessively on her shoulder. "We need some time to talk about us and plan our future. You must stop hounding your brother. He will figure it out."

"Go on with him." Connal seemed to be shooing them away. "I'd like some time with Wynnie if she'll allow it."

"You cannot treat her as if she has always known you and *kens* that you would never hurt her. Wynnie is fragile, along with her heart and soul. I suspect she will give herself to you completely when she comes to love you. But you've got a long road ahead of you. She has only been treated badly by men. In her mind, why should you be any different?" Brenna said as she left with Alistair, his arm wrapped possessively around her shoulder.

Connal inhaled several long breaths of air then seemed to hold it inside before he turned once more to cast his gaze on Wynnie, his wife. Last night seemed to have passed in front of him in a blur, everything happening too fast to comprehend. For the time being the title of wife was in name only and most likely would be for some months to come.

She stood in front of him, her hands clasped tightly in front of her. Her eyes still huge wide terrified pools of blue. "Would you like me to order a bath and food for you?"

"Will you join me in the solar?" he asked, wishing he dared wrap his arm around her as Alistair did his sister. "I would relish more time with you."

"Not for your bath." And he was surprised when she smiled. It seemed genuine and from the heart.

"Are you teasing a bit?" he asked, hoping some time in their not too distant future she would truly share a bath with him and so much more. For now, he would settle for what was right in front of him

For a brief moment, she looked down then decided to meet his gaze. "I was thinking of yesterday when you changed to your cat when I was in the tub. I thought you would jump into the water with me. Didn't think cats liked water but I'm infinitely more comfortable with you in your other form."

He roared with laughter and he stifled it as soon as he noticed the changing expression on her face. "Sorry, lass, that's a misnomer. Big cats love water but I was laughing at the fact you are more at ease with cats than humans. What about you? Do you like to swim? The loch is cold this time of year but invigorating for a short swim. We could go now."

She started walking toward the main hall. He joined her, wondering once more if he said something wrong. He kept his hands at his sides, looking straight ahead. He was terribly worried he would fail at this courting thing.

"I can swim well enough but don't relish freezing water. Don't find anything invigorating about it. Should I wait downstairs until you are through bathing?" She stopped at the steps, looking over her shoulder at the room behind her as if longing to hide there.

"Do you want to remain here?" It seemed to Connal once again she was caught between two things she didn't want to do.

"No, I wouldn't feel at ease. The only person I know besides you is Brenna and she has gone to be with Alistair." Once again, she clasped her hands in front of her while she stared at her feet.

"And you would feel more at ease observing me in my bath?" He wanted to laugh but wisely held the merriment inside. She loathed men but... but what, he wondered. Perhaps she did feel a tiny element of trust when she thought of him. He was fairly confident she enjoyed the two kisses they shared a couple of hours ago.

"Yesterday I would have said nay but today..." She lifted small shoulders, ones that seemed to have carried the weight of the world on them for too many years. He would like nothing more than to take that weight from her shoulders. "Today I would feel more at ease with you," she hesitated then, "even seeing you naked. So far you have not harmed me." Then after a long pause, she said softly, "Your body is..."

He grinned, pleased with her honesty as well as the slender thread of trust she held out to him. Perhaps there was hope for them. "I will set up the privacy screen so you don't have to look upon me."

For a moment she turned away. He would have sworn she was about to object. "That would be nice."

"Only if you don't want to enjoy... my nakedness. It matters not to me." Yet he acknowledged it did matter more than he cared to admit right now.

She moistened her lips before looking down then back to him, seeming to hesitate before saying, "I do like..."

"Your bath is ready." A servant interrupted the conversation. "When we saw you and Alistair fighting in the yard, we anticipated your needs."

"You do that often? Fight?"

"When the mood hits. Fighting each other helps hone our skills." He gave a quick lift to his broad shoulders. "Other things as well."

Connal imagined Wynnie was thankful for the disruption. He was having a hard time picturing her breaking out of her shell quite so quickly as to admit she liked the way he looked naked. Maybe he was wrong. Perhaps that was not what she was going to say.

In silence they walked the rest of the way. He opened the door to his solar and waited for her to pass through. Near the fireplace a huge tub waited for him with steaming water. Clean clothing had been set on the bed for him. For the moment he had just about everything he needed.

"Connal," her voice was whisper thin. "I was going to say you are the most pleasant man to look upon I have ever seen. Perhaps it is because you are not forcing me to have sex with you or mayhap it's because you..." she swallowed hard, "You do not seem to possess any fat."

Then as if totally embarrassed, she walked to the big chair near the fireplace and sat down, her gaze riveted on the floor. He needed her to look at him. Her words brought awe to him.

He appreciated her candid assessment even though it seemed to have embarrassed her. At least he hoped it was honesty unsure of what else it might be. Briefly last night he'd seen her naked. She was slender and possessed beautiful curves. Her breasts would easily fill his hands, if she ever allowed him the closeness. She was willow thin though but her muscles seemed tight. Perhaps some of that came from hiding in the woods and riding. She handled her horse with skill and expertise.

One small touch at a time.

Slipping into the hot liquid he closed his eyes, dreaming dreams of Wynnie and himself lost in the throes of passion. He imagined claiming her and truly making her his, marking her. He wanted her in the most elemental ways, primal and mercurial in nature.

If her father had thoughts that this marriage wasn't valid or real, he was right, but it was much more real than anything that would ever exist between Wynnie and Perkins. If she had not run, Perkins most likely would have never wed her yet he would have continued to use her.

Servants entered with food and drink. He wasn't sure if she wanted to stay ensconced in this room or meet more of their people. Brenna must have introduced her to at least a few of the clan when he and Alistair first began to fight.

He jerked slightly when she stood beside the tub, a glass of ale in her hand, offering the drink to him. She set a table nearby so he had some place to put it.

"Thank you. Did you serve yourself?" he asked, amazed at her actions and wondered why when she was so clearly frightened.

"Thought I should wash your back if you'd like," she murmured, seeming to try to smile. "It is not foreign to me. Was asked to do that numerous times. Every time..."

"I would but I've the feeling it's the last thing you want to do. Why do you ask?" He touched her hand with his, holding her fingers for a second before letting them go.

"I thought you would like me to do it." She soaped a sponge. "You will have to lean forward though. I'll try to be gentle."

"Not until you tell me why. Tell me again so I can fully understand." He studied her expression and could see nothing in her eyes that would tell him anything. They were blank and distant, a place where she must have gone in the past. He didn't want to continue on in this vein. His guess was that she'd been forced to wash the men who forced her.

She sat back then, seeming to focus a bit more on him. "Because they wanted me to and if I did something as simple as washing the man's back after..." she swallowed again, "then..."

"Then what?" he felt a deep and very dark anger begin to simmer inside when he thought of all that happened to her before she fled her home, risking her life.

"Then father *wouldnae* beat me." The words were quick and staccato like as she said them. She closed her eyes as if remembering those times but trying to force them from her head.

"I would rather you tended to me because you wanted to rather than from fear that I would beat you. I won't ever do that, Wynnie."

"So you say. You are a man and men cause pain." She still held the sponge in her hand, but her eyes were no longer hazy.

"Go relax, enjoy something to drink and whatever snack cook sent up. I will be out in a few minutes and dressed. After that we can walk along the parapets. It is my favorite place and you can tell me more about yourself."

"There is not much to tell that you don't already *ken*," she murmured, her head down once again.

He heard the underlying tone that told him what she said wasn't entirely true. She was holding something back, perhaps her hopes and goals, things she had never thought to have. He would love to uncover the truths she didn't want to believe in and teach her that now there was hope.

Ducking beneath the water then standing he poured the bucket of rinse water over him. The tiny amount of water had cooled and he shuddered when the liquid hit his flesh. Surprising him, she was in front of him, a bath towel in hand, giving it to him.

"You don't have to wait on me, lass. I understand that I make you uncomfortable," he said, his voice husky with a growing passion for her he was having a devilishly hard time concealing. He would have to school his baser needs.

"I..." She stepped backwards a few steps, her voice shaking. "Don't want to displease you. You are my husband and important to me."

Guessing the truth of her behavior, "I will not hit you, ever. If nothing else, you need to understand that one fact." Truly he didn't *ken* what it was he needed to do to prove that to her. Time perhaps or would she ever trust him, ever give her heart and soul over to his safekeeping?

Hopefully in time she would do just that.

Quickly he dried off and dressed then extended his arm to her, hoping she would accept. "Shall we go to the battlements? You can look over your land, the land of our clan."

For several moments she held back then seeming to understand this was something he wanted her to do, she hesitantly placed her hand on his arm. He felt the touch all the way to his toes, his body responding.

"My being your wife does not make the land mine. The people will have to accept me first for that to be true." She walked beside him, up the steps until they reached the top. "You *dinna ken* if they will do that."

He led her to the wall where she'd found him early this morning. Where she'd come with Brenna. He'd left her with dangerous and dark frustrations eating at him.

The view of his land always caused his smile to grow. Most of these lands were treeless yet rugged. Mountains pushed to the sky while streams flowed quickly downward in places creating beautiful waterfalls. Cliffs protruded from the hills and heather covered the ground. In some places the soil and the weather were not good for growing plants, but it was good for the clan Chattan.

"Clan Chattan will accept you simply because you are my mate. I *ken* you are sweet and kind. For that reason alone they will come to love you." He realized the truth of his words as he spoke them, even knowing so little about her.

"You can't possibly know that," she murmured, a small smile on her face seeming to form. "We've known each other less than a full day. I could be wickedly evil for all you know."

He chuckled softly, one eyebrow above the other, "Wickedly evil?"

"Yes, what do you know of me except what Perkins and my father told you. I'm sure their words were not laced with honey. They've told others that I was a wild child and needed taming. That sex with me would help me behave and bow down to the ways of men. Sex would teach me how a man wanted to be treated."

His gut churned at her words. If he could slit their throats, he would do it. Torture would be better.

He placed his hand on her waist, thrilled she didn't flinch away from him. Instead she held herself still. Someday soon she would lean into him. Now he understood she simply wanted to keep the status quo because she didn't want to make him angry. She didn't want him to beat her or send her away. She had been willing to just do it, so she would get the sex with him done and over. He would never allow anything so preposterous.

He shuddered thinking about those two men who he considered less than human. "Very few words were exchanged between us. What he told Alistair might be a different story, but my friend has not divulged the gist of their conversation except that Perkins coveted Brenna last night." Which led to Brenna sleeping in the chamber with Alistair for her protection. He needed to remind himself and come to terms with that fact.

"My intended covets everyone in a skirt. I would be surprised if someone in your household was not in his bed last night."

"No one that I've heard of was forced. Perkins and your father would not have been allowed to leave this morning if anything like that had happened."

~ * ~

Wynnie wasn't sure how to proceed with Connal who seemed to

be willing to wait forever to have sex with her. Not for one minute, now that she was getting to know him, did she think he would hurt her on purpose, but she didn't see any other end to sex.

He would have to prove it to her.

She turned to him then, "Truly I would like you to do what men do with their wives tonight. I don't want to put it off any longer than I have to, you know." She was plucking at her skirts and staring fixedly at her feet. "Even though a part of me is terrified, we must make sure there is a child growing in my womb when my father returns. We all know he will."

Connal let out a long slow breath of air, seeming to study her intently. "What about this? Tonight I let you do anything you want with my man's body. You can touch me and kiss me anywhere and anytime you would like. I won't complain and when or if you don't look at me with dazed eyes, perhaps we can take this one step further. It all depends on what I see in your eyes."

She grimaced then walked away, striding to the other side of the battlement, unsure of what all that would entail, touching his man's body. She certainly didn't think she could have sex without retreating to her pleasant place. When she stopped at the wall, he was beside her, leaning against the stones next to her, close to her, but barely touching. She felt a small shiver tease her as well as a tiny wave of heat when he set his hand on her back.

"I wouldn't know how. Don't know what you would like. Never touched a man before." She closed her eyes, trying to imagine what he said, what he'd just given her permission to do.

He shrugged his broad shoulders then running his hand down her back, caressing each tiny bone, "I suppose we are at a stalemate. Either you make love to me, or nothing will happen between us. Do you want a baby?"

"I don't see why. It isn't as if you don't know how or what to do. You are experienced, I'm sure." Anger or perhaps frustration with this stubborn man seemed to simmer in deep dark places inside where she couldn't reach. His soft laughter irritated her even more.

"I'm sorry, lass. It seems I've laughed at your expense." He was gazing into her eyes and she his. Connal's brown eyes seemed to darken with some emotion she knew nothing about.

She wanted to learn though. She also wanted to learn to laugh. Laughing was not something she could remember doing.

Wynnie moistened her lips in expectation of something she wasn't sure of. His grin widened and it seemed he was enjoying the moment. "Look at me, Wynnie. Don't close your eyes."

"Why?" She held her breath, waiting and watching as his mouth slowly caressed hers. The touch was pleasant, something unexpected. She did remember the last time and it was also nice. He pulled away, leaving her gasping for a breath of air.

"Because I want you to always know I'm the man kissing you. If you keep your eyes open you will not be afraid."

"I *dinna ken* why it would be so important. No other man but you has kissed me." She realized she liked his kisses, perhaps even more than she cared to admit. "They seem to make me melt from the inside out and my stomach feels as if it has little butterflies flitting about inside."

"What makes you melt?" he queried, his voice husky and deliciously smooth, warming her.

She punched him on the shoulder wondering if he was purposely being daft. "Kisses, your kisses to be precise. No one else's kisses. Just yours, you horrid man." She crossed her arms in front of her. "Beast."

He moved away then, watching her intensely. "Perhaps this evening you can kiss me so I can feel the same way, melting from the inside out and the butterflies... you say they are flitting about in your stomach? Is that good or bad?"

Disappointed in his answer, she pushed that thought to the back of her head. "I thought you would kiss me again and yes the butterflies are good. You don't feel them?"

"I will kiss you every time you ask or you can kiss me anytime you like. Just say the word. I'll be yours to do with as you please," he said, gently placing a tendril of her fiery red hair behind her ear. "But just not anymore right now. Would you like to go for a ride tomorrow? I'd take you today but until I hear from my people that your father and Perkins have left McKenna land, we should stay inside the castle walls."

"I'd rather not talk of them but of us, you. Do you change to your cat often?" She was curious about him. "I don't *ken* why but I wasn't afraid when you changed right in front of me. I didn't care if your cat saw me with no clothes on. It's different than when you look at me."

"Only when there is some sort of need. The other night I was restless so Alistair as well as my cousins and I went deep into the countryside so we could shift and run. I needed a cold swim in the loch and now I understand why the restlessness took over me. It was leading me to you."

"That's why you were out so late at night. Why you caught me, I guess. If I had known, I would have never fought you. As it was, I believed one of my father's minions had found me. I wanted to die right then. I knew I couldn't go back, but the way you captured me I understood I had no choice." She leaned into him, suddenly feeling more comfortable with the man.

He wrapped an arm around her, drawing her close, comforting and she understood from the way he held her, she could move away from him if she wanted. He would not hold her captive, would never do things she didn't want him to do.

"It was not well done of me."

"What? I'm not understanding." She blinked, confused as to what exactly he was speaking of.

"Tying you and taking you to the tower room. I'm not proud of myself but... Well, I guess there is no excuse." He let out a long heavy breath of air. "Tell me something about yourself."

"Like what?" She felt a smile growing in her heart, something she'd never experienced before.

"Well," he paused thoughtfully, touching the tip of her nose with a fingertip, his perfect white teeth gleaming in the sunlight. "I know the color of your eyes and your hair and that you must not weigh much over one hundred pounds. When were you born?"

"As my father tells me, it was a dark and evil night. My mother left not too many days after I was born. We *dinna* celebrate my birth. When the day would come around, it felt more as if a funeral was taking place rather than a celebration of the day I was born." The lightheartedness she'd felt only a few moments ago vanished in the wake of her memories.

"So you don't know?"

"I didn't say that exactly. I'm assuming it was the fifteenth of May. He would always disappear for the day, cursing my existence and me. I was left to fend for myself and many times..." She didn't want to finish her thoughts, didn't care to remember any of those days.

"Where did he go?"

"He never told me. In any case I never asked. He would usually come back in a better mood. Perhaps he had a woman he saw, a mistress or some poor soul who he would force."

"May fifteenth," he paused, seeming to think, "Do you want to celebrate your birth on that day or should we give you a new birth date, say October twenty-ninth. 'Twas the day I found you. The day could be considered a starting over for you as well as for me. At least I hope it is so."

"I'd like that." Truly she thought his idea was a fine one. "I've never had a real birthday before. When is yours?"

"October twenty-second, lass. I feel as if you were my gift for the year and I need nothing more."

"So, we are each a year older." A cold breeze seemed to sweep off the hills. "I'll be twenty next year." She never thought she would live that long.

He pulled her close, her back against his chest as he held her, his chin resting on the top of her head. She found she liked this man and wondered if this emotion could ever change to love. She'd never thought to like a man let alone love one. Mayhap she was living in a fantastical dream world one that would soon come crashing down around her. Guarding her emotions might be a prudent course of action for the days to come.

She closed her eyes, absorbing the warmth of this man, this very different man in the scope of her experiences. Warm, gentle and kind but in some ways he was a bit rough around the edges. Her father and Perkins were refined and always proper, not Connal. Yet the head of the McKenna clan was so much more a man that the others she'd known.

"We are indeed," he murmured, turning her in his arms and lifting her chin so she was peering into his eyes.

Hers were wide open now and she sensed he was going to kiss her again. She touched her top lip with the tip of her tongue, thinking she'd like to taste him. The thought sent a rush of heat to her cheeks. For a moment she looked away, not wanting him to see.

"My goodness..." She wasn't sure what to say as she felt the whispering warmth of his breath against her cheek. Yet is seemed he didn't miss the rush of color.

"You blush. What are you thinking that causes your cheeks to turn such a beautiful shade of pink?" He swept his lips across her. His were so soft and moist, warm, tantalizing her senses. Her pulse pounded as she could barely catch a breath.

For a moment she lowered her lashes, swallowing and wishing she could tell him without coloring even more.

"Wynnie?" He touched his tongue to her lips, lightly then his lips slanted across hers for a quick kiss. "Tell me."

"If you promise not to laugh," she said, turning her head away for a second then deciding courage and the truth were the best way to proceed.

"Look at me, please." He sighed softly and she wanted to know what he was thinking. "I will never laugh at you, perhaps with you from time to time."

"I think I *ken* that but still..." she paused, plucking at his shirt, unsure why she was touching him and wishing for something more that he could give her but not knowing what that was. "I was thinking, wondering... I'd like to know what you taste like."

Gently, he ran his finger across her mouth, dipped it slowly inside. "After all you've been through in your short life, you unman me. I want to make the rest of your life one of happiness and pleasure yet I cannot promise there will be no difficult times for us. Can you accept that?"

"Don't expect promises or a lifetime of sunny weather. Just kiss me again. Let me taste you this time." She smiled at him, touching the cleft in his chin with the tip of her finger. "I like your kisses. They unravel me, make my knees weak."

"If you want to taste me, you'll have to open your sweet lips for me, give me your tongue. Can you do that?" Slowly he lowered his head.

She heard his groan and wondered at that. "Yes," she murmured as his lips closed over hers. She felt his tongue against her flesh, remembered his words and opened for him. The touch of his tongue inside her mouth, sweeping within amazed her and seemed to heighten all her senses as well as the butterflies in the pit of her stomach. She gripped his shoulders, her fingers tightening as his hands cupped her derriere and pulled her against him.

His arousal against her belly didn't frighten her even though she knew what it meant. The feel seemed to create sensations she didn't understand, never experienced before. Truly, he was nothing at all like the other men she'd known.

Then she found that his kiss deepened and her tongue was playing with his, touching and withdrawing, dancing and dueling. The taste of him swept through her as he tugged her bottom lip with his teeth. She found her knees did not want to function.

He lifted her in his arms, carrying her down the long steps to his chamber. She hoped he would have sex with her now, truly consummate their marriage. His arousal had pulsed against her and while fear should have been the overpowering emotion, it wasn't. For reasons she didn't understand, she wanted him, needed to feel him deep inside her.

She needed to cry out her distress when he sat down on the large chair and not the bed with her on his lap. He continued kissing her though, her face and neck then his teeth tugged on her ear, found a sensitive spot behind it. Little sounds escaped her, rippling from somewhere deep within her lungs. She'd never felt anything so magical and enchanting before this kiss. Her hips seemed to be moving, arching upward as if searching for something and she *kenned* that only he could give it to her.

He stopped then, his breathing heavy as was hers. His head rested on her forehead. "We need to cease before I take this farther than you are ready. I can barely contain myself."

"I want you to kiss me again." Her voice was a thin wail that didn't sound at all like her. "And other things. The things men do."

"If I keep kissing you, we'll be on that bed and I'll be inside you, lass. I don't want to frighten or hurt you. I crave for you to want me as much as I want you. I fear you do not." He was refastening parts of her clothing that had somehow come undone.

Never before had a man set her clothes to rights. Usually they were in tatters when they finished. Truly she was beginning to understand just how different this man was from the others she'd known. He was even putting her hair back into the chignon that seemed to have been falling down around her shoulders.

"I do want you." Her voice cracked when she spoke, but when she looked at the bed, a small lump of dark fear and apprehension settled in her stomach rumbling around, replacing the sweet delicious butterflies.

"Maybe you'll want me more tomorrow," he said, finishing the last touches on her gown and hair. Then his voice husky, he asked, "Shall we have dinner?"

"Dinner?" She couldn't possibly eat. At the moment she was confused and stimulated to a point she didn't understand. It was a novel sensation but she was hot and felt so different.

"Yes, we didn't spend much time downstairs today. Food should be a priority if we want to keep up our strength."

Blindly, she was nodding her head, accepting whatever he said when she really wanted to continue to explore other possibilities between them. Then reluctantly, "I suppose we could go downstairs."

He set her off his lap, a too broad grin on his handsome face to suit her, thinking he was up to something. Her legs were wobbly. She was relieved when he offered his arm. She leaned on it for support.

In the hall, she saw the few people she did know: his cousins, Angus and Fergus, his sister and Alistair. They sat at a table, chatting together, laughing. A fire burned in the fireplace, a cheery glow encompassing the scene. A small dog lay by the fire soaking up the heat while a cat was curled next to his head.

All around children were, with the help of their parents, carving lanterns out of turnips for gaizin on all hollows' eve. The children were preparing their masks and the lanterns for their visits to houses.

She smiled. All had been similar at her home near Glasgow.

He escorted her to his cousins and reintroduced her. They were with him the other night when he found her and brought her to the castle, as was Alistair. He led her around the keep presenting her to various people and as the list grew, she knew she would be unable to remember the names.

When he was done and she was thoroughly confused, he pulled up two chairs by his sister and Alistair. True to form he left her with his sister once more. It seemed he didn't feel like eating any more than she did. She watched his retreating back and wondered if he was going to shift and run again. She certainly wished she could do something to ease her frustration.

~ * ~

Oscar took his irritations out on Heather, Wynnie's mother. He always did. Whenever Wynnie escaped his plans by fleeing into the woods, he would come to this hovel where he kept her mother.

He fastened his pants, watching Heather. She was always stoic. Had not been the first time he had sex with her. If Heather had ever shown a sign that she enjoyed his company, he might have kept her in a better place, somewhere she could live more easily.

From the first time, she fought him. He'd grown to like that side of her though, relished the few times he watched Wynnie try to fight the men he brought to her. It was always arousing. The resistance was part of the charm. When Wynnie began to withdraw from herself, that was when he decided to sell her to others besides Perkins.

The girl eluded him. While he told her he didn't know if she was his, those words had been a lie. Wynnie was his even though she looked just like her mother.

"Where is Wynnie?" she asked. "You always speak of her when you come, just to taunt me. I understand but..."

Anger simmered deep inside in the darkest places. He waved a hand. "She fled."

A smile formed on Heather's face. "Do you know where she is? Is she safe?"

"Safe enough. She took refuge at the McKenna's castle in northern Scotland. The McKenna says he is wed to her but the only proof of that was the fact she was in his bed."

"She is safe for now and my heart is glad."

"Perhaps I could hold your life over her head. She would come to me if she thought it would save her mother's life." He was pacing and rubbing his chin deep in thought.

"She won't believe you. The ruse you played with her was too true and thorough for her to think you lied all those years. She has believed I'm dead for a very long time."

"You might be right, but it won't stop me from trying."

~ * ~

"How long do I have to wait for my husband to believe I'm ready to be a wife in all ways?" Wynnie asked Brenna. "It's been over a month. He was the one who said I needed to be with child as soon as possible. He kisses me then finds ways to ignore me. I am ready but he doesn't believe what I tell him. Stubborn man."

Brenna's heart went out to Wynnie. It seemed to her, Wynnie tried every way imaginable to convince Connal of that fact.

"I think I've a way he won't be able to resist you." Brenna said linking her arm through Wynnie's as they strolled in the garden. "But you will have to put aside your inhibitions. Courage, my dear."

Wynnie stopped, turning toward her, "Really? I've talked and talked. He won't listen to me. He will kiss me and make me feel hot and..." She was shaking her head, trying to tell Brenna everything, all the sensations.

"I *ken* what you're feeling."

"Do you? But," she paused, "Alistair makes love to you. He doesn't just kiss and make the butterflies dance in your belly."

"He does but I didn't come to him abused by people I should have been able to trust. Connal doesn't want to hurt you. He's afraid that if he does, you'll never trust him again."

"So, just what is this notion of yours? I'm ready to become his wife in every way." She stopped to look over the yard. "He and Alistair have been fighting now almost daily. I do believe Alistair is getting tired of the battles."

"First of all, they do need to keep their battle skills sharpened. And second, if you want to make it impossible for your man to keep his hands to himself, all you need do is present yourself to him without a stitch of clothing on." Brenna took Wynnie's hands in hers, "I know it will seem awkward at first but you can do it. I know you can."

"How? He comes in late at night, dons his night shirt and crawls into the far side of that huge bed."

"He doesn't even give you a kiss goodnight?" Brenna asked, slowly dropping Wynnie's hands.

"He only kisses me when he knows it can't go any farther. We go to the parapets and he kisses me until I can't stand any longer. Then he will run any loose strands of my hair through his fingers. Sometimes he lets out a long-discontented sigh."

"That does not sound like the rumors that have always flourished about my brother. He has always been a lady's man, quick to bed a willing lass who might catch his fancy. He must really love you."

"Love? What is love? I certainly have never felt love from any human. Indeed, you and Connal are the only people who I even like." Wynnie hesitated for a second. "I did like the elderly woman who used to hide me from father. Her name was Berta."

"First, you need to stay awake until he comes to bed. Second, all you need do is wear, say a robe with nothing on beneath it. When Connal comes in and disrobes for bed, you should walk up to him and slip the robe off your shoulders. He will not be able to resist the temptation. I promise you, Wynnie, the ploy will work."

"You promise it will work." Wynnie's hands were shaking as she questioned Brenna's words. "I would be mortified if he rejected me."

Brenna smiled, squeezing Wynnie's hands. "He will not reject you. I promise you, whenever you garner the courage to present yourself to your husband without a stitch of clothing on, he will make love to you. I promise. The act will tell him all that he's been waiting to hear from you. It will be more than words that will convince him. It will be your actions."

It seemed to Brenna that Wynnie mulled her words over in her head for the longest time. "Courage, that is what I need."

"You can do it. I know you can," Brenna whispered. "Come, the day is growing late. We should get back inside. Do it tonight while you cannot come up with reasons to gainsay yourself."

Chapter Five

Connal finished the ale he was drinking before striding to the parapets to look over the land. It was the first snow of the season and the middle of December. He had yet to make love to Wynnie although he *kenned* she wanted him. He was terrified he would hurt her. Terrified that somehow his actions would cause her to draw away from him.

Yet he was afraid, terribly afraid he would hurt her and ruin everything.

The cowardice in him surfaced every time he thought of her eyes and the way they assumed a vague hue when he touched her. Granted it had been a month or more since he'd seen that vacant stare, but the memory haunted his soul and reminded him of the abuse she lived through at her father's hands, a man who should have protected her. She told him she wanted him to make love with her. He wanted to believe her.

He looked up as the flakes touched his face and melted, wondering if Wynnie enjoyed the snow. In the morning he would have to find out. Perhaps they could go for a short ride into the hills. Would she even know how to play in the snow? Had she ever had the chance? So many questions and most of them he didn't ask not wanting to remind her of times better left in her memories.

His words about a quick pregnancy came back to haunt him. She was not, could not, unless he made love to her. Except for her sake and the status of their marriage, he didn't care. God willing, children would happen in their own time. He gritted his teeth, attempting to control his unruly body that seemed to harden every time he thought of her naked and in the bed waiting for him. That one glimpse of her was not enough.

This was not the way to go forward with this marriage. Perhaps he should make love to her in the dark so he wouldn't be able to see into her eyes. "You are a dimwitted fool, Connal McKenna, if you think you wouldn't feel her body stiffen in fear beneath you."

Inhaling a long and deep breath of air and tormented by his thoughts, he turned toward the stairway leading downward, determined to make it through another night of celibacy, lying beside her and wishing for so much more. He'd even taken to wearing a damn nightshirt. At the door he paused, his hand on the latch. Closing his eyes, he drank heavily of the air he could absorb into him before entering. What he needed was a miracle.

A soft candle lit room presented itself to him, lights flickering all around. Gently, he closed the door, leaning against it, his gaze roamed the room, searching for the reasons. His stomach wrenched in sudden fear that something was very wrong.

"Wynnie? Is everything alright?" he asked as he stepped further inside wondering at the candles and the soft glow seeming to warm the room even while the fire had been built up. Perhaps nothing was wrong and mayhap she was just having trouble falling asleep.

"I'm fine." Her voice was soft, sounding different to his ears, almost compelling.

"Good then, you should go back to sleep." He slipped out of his shirt, his back muscles flexing when he felt her presence behind him. Felt her soft hand on his shoulder.

"Connal?" Her hand rested on his back, caressed softly, enticed and he knew she didn't mean the gesture. A groan rumbled from deep inside as his entire body hardened with need. "You should go back to bed." He spoke through gritted teeth straining to control his aroused body.

"*Dinna* want to."

He turned then, a gasp rasping from his lungs. "Wynnie..." She was standing in front of him with nothing covering her. Her hands were on the fastening of his kilt. He touched her trembling fingers, wishing he understood what she was about. Since that first night when they wed, he had not seen her naked. Now she stood in front of him with nothing on, not a stitch. She was the most beautiful sight in all his life. He couldn't swallow, couldn't breathe. He was sure his heart forgot to beat.

She moistened her lips, "Tonight, please... I want more than a kiss. I want you to make love to me. I want to *ken* what it feels like when you are deep inside me, loving me as only you can."

"*Ach*, but you're not ready, lass." His voice rasped from his lungs. He could barely speak let alone think. "My god but you're beautiful. I could never forgive myself if I hurt you."

"You won't."

"You don't know that."

The glow from the soft light of the candles seemed to highlight the rounded globes of her breasts as well as the gentle curve of her hips. "You should take the rest of your clothes off," she whispered. "I'll help if you like."

Had he really stayed away from her all of these weeks? She wanted him, had told him many times. Yet he continued to believe she would be terrified of him. This woman was not afraid, perhaps she only pretended, but he'd also told her there would be only pleasure. Her fingers fumbled with his clothing.

"Let me do that." He groaned again as her fingers brushed against aroused, pulsing flesh.

"You will have sex with me then?" Her smile was small and hesitant.

He guessed she wasn't entirely sure of what she was asking and it was now up to him to show her there was a difference between forced sex and making love. "I will." He was naked now. He scooped her into his arms, carrying her to the bed where the covers were already pulled back, waiting for them.

In his arms, he felt the hardening tips of her breasts as they scraped against him, rubbed temptingly. The weight of making this right for her pushed harshly on his shoulders. On the bed he came down beside her, tracing her collarbone with the tip of one finger, trying to figure out just how he should proceed.

She moistened her lips, her small pink tongue enticing him with the warmth it offered, yet he understood the delicacy of this situation. His lips brushed against hers, once then twice. She responded sweetly but with hesitation; still so much an innocent in this.

"Are you going to torture me first?" she asked, her hands resting on his chest. "I like the way you feel, Connal, but my body seems to be burning for you, for your touch. I've never known anything like this."

The groan rumbled up from deep in his chest. "I like the way you feel too, lass, *mo shiorghra.*" *My eternal love*, he murmured. His mouth closed hungrily over hers, gently at first then the fire and the spirit of the night seemed to take over his heart. The sweet magic enchanted him. The inferno had been building since that day in October when he held her behind him on his horse and her body was flush against his.

She fought him then and he didn't understand why, couldn't comprehend why he acted the way he did. Perhaps there was truly a reason for everything.

When he pulled away, he needed to see into her eyes. They were wide open, a bit of awe and wonder in them but clear and cognizant of everything he was doing. She trusted him. He could read it in her eyes. Could see the sweet innocence that was Wynnie. He sensed the heat of her body against his, the curve of her thighs against him and knew she felt his arousal, pulsing against her.

Yet she didn't pull away from him.

Lightly he touched her breast, keeping his gaze upon her. He drew his fingers low over her ribs then against her belly, down her thighs. Her lashes fluttered lightly across her cheeks. "Are you sure, lass?" he asked her softly, and she lifted her gaze to his again as he invaded her more intimately. She drew her limbs together as the flames of his caress must be touching her. Yet her body surged against his caress. He laughed with sheer pleasure as his lips seized upon hers.

"I've never been more sure of anything," she sighed then the whisper of her breath stroked his cheek, "but you have to tell me what you want, what to do?"

"Candlelight," he told her. "Thank God that you craved the light, for whatever reason because I hunger for the sight of you and desire whatever you are willing to give this night. I'm so glad you chose to look at me too."

His lips covered hers again and again then growing bolder they traveled lower, in tempest and wild abandon to her breasts and ever lower to her belly. Brazenly, he touched the softest part of her. Her honey flowed. She cried out loud, stunned by the intimacies he was taking with her. His touch like this was most likely nothing she'd ever felt before, and he prayed he was not hurting her.

He was determined in this to give her pleasure and vanquish the fears that possessed her for so many years. He teased her no longer but fell upon her with purpose, parting her thighs to his desire, cradling her gently in his arms. He knew there would be no virgin's pain, but he didn't know how small and tight she was.

Easing inside her, he slowly stretched her, felt the heat and moisture that flowed for him, for the pleasure he was sure would follow. She was breathing heavily, her hips rising to meet him, drawing him ever deeper into her velvet warmth. She wanted him and it pleased him.

"It's alright. You won't hurt me." Her fingers were biting into his shoulders.

He continued to stroke her and kiss her until she was mindlessly moving against him. She closed her eyes. He allowed it for a moment. Then, "Open your eyes, sweet lass. I want to see you when I give you your first pleasure."

Tremors seemed to sweep from her and into him. "Connal!" she cried out his name as he surged ever deeper inside, harder and faster. All consuming tremors encompassed her.

He groaned and thrust one more time, feeling the release of his seed. "Wynnie." Exhausted, he whispered her name. The magic of the moment eclipsed him, seared into him as the darkness around his heart and soul lifted and was replaced with the light he'd always craved.

Rising above her, he brushed damp hair from her eyes, concern for her overriding all else. He braced his weight on his forearms but he still felt the tips of her breasts against his chest. He smiled, pleased with himself and what just happened between them.

"I had no idea," she spoke softly, touching his cheek, running a fingertip along his jaw. "I believe you now. Only pleasure."

His heart went out to her. Where lovemaking with Wynnie was concerned, he realized his goal by showing her it wasn't all about pain and domination. Now he prayed their lives would continue on a more even keel. Still, they needed to brace against the return of her father and intended. He had not claimed her. Had not wanted to inflict any pain tonight. Marking her in the way of the clan Chattan would wait for another time, a time when he could explain to her what would happen and how they would once again be joined for eternity.

He rolled to his side, pulling her close, her head and one hand resting on his chest. "I'd like to know what you are thinking."

"That you are not like the others. Your shoulders are broad and bronzed from the sun even though winter is nearly upon us. Everything about you is masculine and if I didn't know you so well, intimidating. When I first saw you, you stole my breath."

He laughed at her words, having never thought that way about himself. "It was snowing before I came to my room. Do you like the snow?"

She pushed away, her hair falling over her shoulders and tickling him. "It is always cold. Winter was a time when men were bored and it was harder for me to hide. Sometimes I could not get away. I always dreaded the first snow fall of the season."

"That is all done now. You should not think of those things again. Perhaps I can teach you how to enjoy the white stuff falling from the sky."

"What if father returns? What will we do?"

To his delight she was kissing him, light small caresses along his chest, sipping with her lips, teasing with her teeth. "You're playing with fire, lass." He was sure it was too soon to make love to her again but if she kept up the evocative and mercurial caresses, he wouldn't be able to control his unruly body.

"How so?" She smiled at him and by the expression in her eyes, he was sure she knew exactly what she was about.

He thought showing her might be easier than explaining. Bringing her hand to his heavy sex, he delighted in her small gasp of surprise before asking. "You *ken* now?"

"So soon?" She pushed against him, smiling at him. "If you want, I suppose... I would not say *nay*." Her teeth pulled her lip into her mouth as she stared at his heavy arousal.

When she turned her attention back to him, he groaned at her expression. "I can wait until..." He wasn't sure if he could wait until tomorrow or the day after that, not even the next ten minutes. He wanted her, needed her in so many ways. How he abstained for well over a month amazed him.

"Why should you postpone?" She kissed his chest lightly, swirling her tongue around a nipple. "Do you like that? You have to tell me, you know. I've no idea what a man likes and what he doesn't. I've never touched a man before you."

"Little minx, are you trying to seduce me? Of course I like what you are doing." He laughed softly, enjoying everything about her and willing to let her do anything she wanted to his man's body.

"I wouldn't know how but..."

"For not knowing you are doing an amazingly fine job." Her lips once more touched him, swept across his lips as she rose against him. Unable to resist, he cupped her breasts in his hands, loving the way they filled them. Then his hands were on her waist, lifting her to straddle him.

"Is this...?" She looked down, saw his rod nestled between her thighs. "Do you... what is it you want?"

"A way to make love," he prompted her, once more watching the ever changing expression on her face. "Any time you like you can put me inside you. It's your decision."

"Any time I like and what would I do?" she questioned even though he'd pretty much just told her and he was sure she was thinking and coming to some conclusions all on her own.

Answering her was not something he planned on doing. She was going to have to figure this one out by herself. His fingers rolled her taut pink nipples gently between them. Then he pulled her closer, sucking them into his mouth, worrying each one alternately with his teeth then tongue. He groaned, feeling the tempest rise within him faster than he ever thought possible. His hands circled her tiny waist then stroked over her hips before caressing her even more intimately. A little mew of pleasure filled her throat as she tossed her head behind her, arching her back, her hair tumbling gloriously around her, touching upon his chest.

It seemed she realized what he wanted and was slowly settling on him. She gazed down at him, her tangled red hair falling in disarray around him. The magic and the enchantment of the night seemed to increase. The tempest soared within him as she moved slowly at first.

"*Ach*, lass, you are in control. Let the sensations rise and grow until you can tolerate no more." She did and minutes later she lay against him, her skin damp with a fine sheen of moisture.

He ran his hands along her back, calming the storm that swept through them. The night would be short, he realized, because he could not get enough of his wife. She wove a web of fascination around him, his wife, his mate for eternity. His *mo shiorghra*.

"I *dinna* feel in control of anything," she sighed softly, still lying on top of him. "I cannot move and I do hope I'm not too heavy for you."

"No, it seems neither of us has any wits about us." He laughed again, pleased with the events of this night. He was a man well pleased by his wife and he hoped she was delighted as well.

He settled her close, listening to the soft cadence of her breaths as she slept. She was nestled against him, her back against his chest while he cupped her breast in a hand. With his wife he found heaven tonight.

On the morrow he should meet with Alistair and lay strategies for the spring. Her father would not come in the winter but when the sun began to shine and travel would not be life threatening. The pair would try to take back what they considered theirs.

They wouldn't succeed.

If his initial plans came to fruition, both Oscar and Perkins would vanish at the Kinnel stones just as Maurina had and just as all the enemies of the clan Chattan. He didn't know how or why, but the place was magical, and people didn't return after entering inside the circle.

When he came to bed this evening, he never expected his wife to seduce him. Brenna must have had something to do with this. He had been so caught up with his life he forgot about the urgent need for Alistair and Brenna to wed. He assumed they would have handfasted but he wanted her wed, the ceremony more binding these days. He would have to put the wedding in motion, assuming there would be no objections.

Wynnie pushed against him, seeming to want more warmth. He grinned. They made love three times before she finally fell asleep and perhaps they would again before he left the bedchamber. For the first time in years, he felt lighthearted. The weight he'd shouldered since Maurina showed her true self vanished.

He claimed Wynnie the last time they made love. The tiny marks on her shoulders would heal quickly and they caused her little pain. He told her what would happen and she agreed.

The banging on the door startled him and woke Wynnie. She sat up, covers falling to her waist and pushing her hair back, "What is it?"

"Cover up," He strode to the door and opened it before taking a long look at Wynnie. "This had better be important."

Alistair was in the hall with fist raised to knock again. "A visitor downstairs."

~ * ~

"One person?" Connal asked, raking his hands through his hair even while he dressed. "That's odd this time of year."

"Only one, and I believe it's a woman," Alistair said, grinning as he spoke and peering in the direction of the bed. "The men woke me first. For some reason they were loathe to bother you. Now I see why. The lady says she came to speak with Wynnie."

"Who do you think she is and why does she want to speak with me? I don't know anyone and except for your sister I don't have any friends," Wynnie asked, wishing she dared go with them and see for herself. "I don't know anyone save Father and Perkins who would want to talk to me. I certainly don't have any acquaintances." She was thinking of the elderly lady who used to help hide her from her father but the lady was far too fragile to make such a trip.

Connal turned to her, his eyes ablaze with emotions. She needed to see into his mind but she was afraid. "Get dressed and meet me in the keep. By the time you get there, we should know who is knocking at our door. Friend or foe, in any case."

She was nodding, her body trembling so hard she wasn't sure if she could move let alone dress herself. *It's a woman, not father or Perkins. I have no reason to be afraid.* "I will." She watched him leave, her fingers plucking at the covers, wishing nothing had come their way to disturb their morning.

Touching her lips, they had been well kissed and her muscles seemed to ache, she supposed, from the activity of last night that she wasn't used to. She needed his arms around her, sheltering her from the elements she understood were hurtling down upon her. This woman had to be the first of Oscar's ploys to take her away from the McKenna.

"May I come in?" Brenna poked her head around the corner of the door, smiling as if she knew something she shouldn't. "I've ordered a bath for you. I know Connal wanted you to come to the keep as soon as possible but I assumed," she paused and shrugged. "After our talk last night, I supposed perhaps you had the courage to go through with my brother's seduction and you would relish a few moments to think about last night and soak in some scented hot water."

"We've had that same talk every night for the last few weeks." Wynnie reminded her as she slipped into the tub. "What makes you think I carried through with your advice?"

"I understand that but you were different last eve, more determined and you seemed desperate to convince him you were ready to become his wife." Brenna busied herself with the breakfast scones that had been brought to the room then poured cups of tea. "I sensed you were afraid you might lose the stubborn man if you didn't do something desperate to keep him."

"You're right of course," Wynnie murmured. "I was desperate and I did take your advice."

"So, the two of you actually made love. I'm happy for you."

The bath was hot and steaming. Wynnie picked up the scented soap then uttered a small sigh as the heat of the water eased her muscles. "I'm tired, no exhausted. I think it would have been nice to sleep the morning away, just laze away beneath the warm covers while Connal held me close. If I'm not mistaken, Connal planned on just that."

Brenna sat on the hearth, her legs crossed, nibbling on a scone, her teacup close by. "So, it happened more than once?"

"Three times and I think he would have made love to me again if Alistair had not interrupted. I was wrapped in his arms and..." Wynnie would never forget the night, the tempest and the magic.

"No pain? Even when he put his mark on you?" Brenna asked. "I know it's not my business and of course you don't have to answer."

"Only when he claimed me. That was only for a second and that too vanished." She looked at one shoulder and saw the tiny marks. "Is it really true am I his mate for all time? Have we been wed before?"

"Aye, tis true. No man can separate the two of you, not your father or Perkins, not even death. The two of you will always find your way back to each other." Brenna stood, wandering the room, seeming restless.

"You need a wedding," Wynnie said, eyeing Brenna as she paced, picking up items then setting them back always in a different spot. "You and Alistair deserve a real wedding as well as a celebration of the nuptials. Winter is a wonderful time for just that sort of thing. A celebration such as that will warm everyone's hearts."

"You and Connal need a celebration also. He is the laird after all and head of the clan Chattan. Our people want him to be happy. They want to show their respect. It's not right the ceremony was done in such haste and the clan was not there to rejoice with the two of you."

"No, it was not," Wynnie sighed, rising from the water and wrapping a towel around her. "We must forget all that and see who has arrived and if this woman poses some kind of threat to me or your clan."

"Our clan," Brenna corrected.

"Yes, I suppose I am part of it now. Before last night I really didn't feel as if I belonged."

"I'm sure all will be fine with the woman. My brother should have

94

made love to you sooner," Brenna said as she helped Wynnie dress. "If I had not shown up, I truly don't see how you could have put all this clothing on by yourself. Connal left in such a hurry with no concern for you, expecting you to arrive downstairs in an appropriate amount of time, properly dressed as well."

"If you had not come on your own, he might have sent you upstairs to help me," Wynnie said.

"If he passed me in the hall, mayhap. Truly the man should get you a ladies' maid. You need one with all your increasing duties. Now that you have a wardrobe you cannot possibly dress without considerable help. Connal, at times, is obviously too busy. I will not always be around to help. Although I'm sure he would rather undress you than dress you now that you two have solved your minor problem as husband and wife."

"Today, yes, of course you are right, but I don't want some lady I don't know helping me put on my clothes. It would be awkward." Wynnie smoothed her skirts thinking about all Brenna told her. "Even after a month I barely know anyone. In my home, I tried to stay away from people. Talking to people is just not something I *ken* how to do. It seems I'm always at a loss for words."

"You should pick her out yourself. Someone you feel comfortable around," Brenna said. "I'll introduce you to some suitable girls who would love to be given such an opportunity then you can spend time with them, perhaps have tea. I will tell them one of the qualifications for the job is putting you at ease."

"Someone my age?" Wynnie asked feeling for the first time that another person to talk with would be nice. "Conceivably someone I could confide in beside you."

"I'm not enough?" Brenna asked in a huff then chuckling. "It is always nice to have more than one confidant. I grew up here, have girlhood friends and we share most everything."

"Of course you are enough. It's just that so many times you are with Alistair. You do have a life and you are not someone who needs employment as a maid. However, I'm very grateful for your assistance today and all the other days that Connal left before he could help me."

"All the days you didn't want him to see you without clothing," Brenna laughed and Wynnie enjoyed the sound.

"After last night I no longer have that excuse. He, well, it seems." She was at a loss for the right words. "I still won't parade around the room without anything on."

"Touched and kissed every inch of you if my guesses are right. There is no need to blush. Alistair has done the same to me. He seems to like it when I lose control and scream his name when he gives me my woman's pleasure as he calls what he does to me. The scream strokes his manly sensibilities."

"Yes, well, I did the same with Connal and you say he must have liked that?" she queried, trying to remember his reaction, but it seemed only a few minutes later he was deep inside her again.

"Of course he did, a man likes that kind of thing. As I implied earlier, it makes them swell with manly pride," Brenna laughed, putting the finishing touches on her hair. "You are more than presentable but are you ready to meet your husband downstairs, understanding the entire clan will know what transpired between the two of you last night?"

Wynnie felt a wave of heat sweep through her to settle on her cheeks. "How would they know something like that? He wouldn't tell anyone would he?" Wynnie wasn't at all sure about what Brenna was saying to her.

"Because even though Alistair ripped him from his bed when he was about to make love to you for a third time or was it a fourth time, there was an undeniable grin on his face, the look of a man well satisfied," Brenna looked smug and too sure of herself. "My brother never grins."

"What does a grin have to do with anything?" Wynnie was more confused than ever.

"The man has been called a brooding monster for the last few years. If he comes downstairs grinning, it can only mean one thing. He's had a night of loving with his beautiful wife," Brenna laughed again, clearly enjoying herself and the wisdom she was imparting to Wynnie.

"Was that because of sex?" Wynnie truly needed explanations into her husband's behavior and the things that left him grinning versus brooding. He never really seemed to brood around her but neither did he grin.

Her husband. He was now her husband in every way. Was grinning. She felt suddenly very pleased with herself.

"Are you ready to see who this woman is?" Brenna asked.

Wynnie held her breath for a moment before letting it out in a soft whoosh. "I suppose I have to." Curiosity seemed to be overpowering the need to stay hidden away in this room.

"Then let's go." Brenna linked her arm through Wynnie's. "What possible harm could come of it?"

A few minutes later they entered the main hall and stopped. Wynnie saw Connal first. He'd been talking to Alistair and when he saw her, he strode toward her, a smile on his face.

"*Ach*, you look very beautiful today." He pulled her into his arms, kissing her full on the lips before deepening the kiss and lifting her off the ground. Connal had never done such a thing and it stole her breath. She wanted the sweet kiss to never end.

He set her on the ground, pushing a few strands of hair behind her ear, his grin heating her through to the core. "You are my wife and all of the clan's resources are available to you. Don't ever forget that," he whispered, his voice raw with emotion. "I suspect you will want to speak with the woman who arrived via an Adair coach, but I don't think she poses a threat to you. At least not at the moment, but you must proceed cautiously."

Wynnie didn't know how to reply and wondered at the urgency in his voice then the softness. He was preparing her for something and trying to give advice the best he could. "What is it you're not telling me?"

He nodded toward a slender redheaded woman. "She says she is your mother. Is it true?"

Wynnie gasped, startled by news she never expected. Then she looked in the direction Connal indicated. "I wouldn't know as she was supposed to be dead. She was taken from me before I have any memories of her. As I grew up, I was forbidden to speak of her. Even her name eludes me. Perhaps I never knew it."

"You look a lot like her," he told her, his voice soft. "Would you like to meet her? Perhaps if you talk to her, you will be able to *ken* if she is your mother or not. If you don't want to acknowledge her in any way, I'll send her back. Although I *ken* she is terrified of returning."

"I'm not in a hurry. If she could travel here in the beginning of winter, she has means. Why didn't she ever try to get me away from Father? Why didn't she help me or even inquire about my wellbeing?"

"That is something you can ask her. Besides, you only have your father's word she did not ask about you. Her name is Heather and yes, she arrived in a carriage. The driver left saying he wouldn't stay. His orders were to leave Heather here and return home."

"Who gave him those orders?" Wynnie was watching the woman sip her tea and delicately taste a scone. She was regal in her bearing and she couldn't be very old. perhaps late thirties. If that were true, it would mean she was very young when she gave birth. Her father had a penchant for younger women.

"He didn't say but I assume it was Adair since the coach had his shield on it." Connal held her hand in his, gently kissing the back. "I will stay by your side. Have courage, lass. The woman doesn't seem to mean you harm. Her health seems to be fragile as well."

"Yes, I would like that. I have so many questions if she is my mother. But I'm terrified to ask. What if she hated me? What if she knew what Oscar did to me?" Wynnie was sure though, Oscar had something if not all to do with her mother's disappearance and her young age spoke to her age when she was pregnant with her. It also spoke of her father's continuing treachery.

When she sat down across from the woman, there was no doubt in her mind that Heather was indeed her mother. She was looking at a mirror image of herself. She smiled then, thanking the stars above she had little of her father in her, especially his character.

Still, just because the woman was indeed her mother, didn't mean the lady didn't intend harm. Oscar might be holding some threat over the woman's head. Because of her absence, she had been through more than a little girl turned woman should be put through. Perhaps Heather's life had been no different.

"Why should I believe you're my mother?" She wanted to see into this woman's soul and hear why she left her daughter in the hands of Oscar Adair. Heather must have known what the man was like and the evil surrounding him.

"You shouldn't but I am. Your father sent me here to find out whatever I could about you and the stronghold. He wants me to betray you and if you want to send me home, then do so." When she set her teacup on the saucer, her hands where shaking.

"Are you going to do that? Give me back to Oscar who sold me to men to do whatever they pleased with me." Wynnie wasn't going to fall into this trap and neither would Connal.

Heather gasped, seeming startled by her revelation. She looked away and when she returned her gaze, there were tears in her eyes. "I *dinna* think he would do that to you, his daughter. I should have known better but in any case, there was nothing I could have done to stop him."

"You could have been there for me," Wynnie was breathing hard, her anger at this woman who abandoned her grew more intense with each second. She couldn't stand to look at her.

Heather reached out to her but Wynnie jerked her hands into her lap, looking away as she tried to keep the tears from turning to sobs.

"He locked me away," Heather blurted, her own tears sliding down her cheeks. "I was a prisoner in the very home where you lived. Oscar never told me anything about you."

"The third floor room? I was forbidden to go there." She remembered the conversations at an early age. By the time she was older and might have defied him, she chose to hide other places, never venturing to the top floor.

"You would have found a locked door, nothing more. In any case, I would not have answered a knock. He kept me drugged most of the time, except when he wanted me then he wanted me wide-awake. Told me he didn't like making love to a corpse, but I never considered what he did as making love." Her bitterness was obvious.

"Did he force you too?" Wynnie blurted, wishing she had not

asked when she saw the expression on Heather's face. "Never mind, I recognize that look of despair. Why would you help him bring me back?"

She slowly shrugged, a faraway expression on her face then inhaling deeply, "If Connal will not protect me, I will suffer Oscar's wrath as well as any man who wants me if I *dinna* do as he commands. Oscar is an evil man as well you must know."

Wynnie glanced at Connal who seemed distracted now by the children playing nearby. "I'm sure my husband will not send you back to Oscar. You must not betray us though."

"But will he protect me?" Heather asked, her eyes wide. "I would rather die than go back to that man and his friends."

"I understand all too well your fears, but I cannot speak for my husband. He will do what he thinks best. Which means he will probably shelter you. He is a good and kind man." Wynnie prayed she was right but only time as well as Heather's actions would tell what he would do. A few tears did not mean the woman who claimed she was her mother was loyal to clan Chattan.

She felt Connal's presence behind her and wondered then what he overheard as well as his intentions. "As long as you are honest and true, the McKenna castle will be your home as well as your sanctuary. You need not fear the man. Is Oscar still your husband?"

She inhaled a swift deep breath, holding for a second, then, "He never was my husband. We didn't wed."

"Then I'm illegitimate, a bastard. Are you sure Oscar is my father? He told me many times he thought I was a bastard which was why I wasn't worthy of a respected place in his household, yet he sought to wed me to a wealthy laird. It never made sense to me."

"You are his but of course a bastard also. It wasn't until after I gave birth to you that he sold me to other men. Over the years he has not changed, will never change." Her voice was whisper thin and filled with emotion that tugged at Wynnie's heart.

Connal's hand settled on her shoulder, reassuring her, making her believe one day this would all be over.

~ * ~

Heather had never felt so alone and out of place. At first, he kept her in a small home near the castle. As time went by though, he decided she needed to live closer to him. Since then she'd been locked away for almost twenty years. Her only contact with the countryside was through a locked window three stories above ground. When she was younger, she harbored thoughts of escaping out that window but Oscar seeming to guess her intent had it painted shut. At the age of thirty-five she wondered what had happened to her life and how it had gone so terribly wrong.

Oscar Adair was what happened to her and she kenned she would never get those lost years back.

Now she looked across a table at a distrustful daughter, one she was never allowed to hold not even the first seconds after giving birth. Guessing now that Oscar had mapped out Wynnie's life the moment he saw her.

"I think Oscar had plans for you from the very moment he discovered you weren't a boy. He might have wed me if I'd given him a son." She tapped her fingers on the table, wondering about the hell he would have put her through if they were married and if it could have been any worse than the one she endured.

"Now at least he has no hold over you," Wynnie said, her voice soft, calming Heather's rattled nerves. "I need to speak with Connal. Will you be alright?" Wynnie asked as she stood.

"I'm fine. I've been given a room. Alistair told me once I spoke with you, I could retire there whenever I wanted. But I suppose I should stay here for the rest of the afternoon. What would I do alone in a room except brood? Maybe someone will be brave and talk with me. Not sure what I would say though..." She lifted her shoulders, searching the room.

"I'll send Brenna over if I see her. She's Connal's sister and she likes to talk to people."

"I certainly understand your reticence. You don't need to send anyone here for me or to keep me company. I'm used to listening to my thoughts," Heather murmured, understanding she'd spent the better part of twenty years entertaining herself. It seemed the present would be no different.

As the hours passed, she found she enjoyed watching the people; servants, children and the more prestigious members of the clan. Watching something other than the walls was new to her. Several of the servants stopped by from time to time to see if she needed anything.

Just time, all she needed was time with her daughter. Yet she knew the years she lost could never be regained. She prayed too that Wynnie would find a way in her heart to forgive her as well as what had been done to her when she had no mother to protect her.

Heather had always thought if she had done things differently or been better in some way, her life would have turned out differently. She sighed long and deep, knowing that wishing and praying would not solve any of her problems. All she could do was forge ahead and make her future better than her past.

"Hello, lass, it's a *bonny* good day today. I'm Elliott Frasier and I've brought you a pint and a basket of bread. More is on the way. I've a powerful hunger. Hope you like it. May I sit?"

She inhaled a deep breath, startled by the man seeming to appear from nowhere. "If you like." She had no idea how to respond to the man or his invitation. He was tall and broad of shoulders. His darkly stubbled chin did nothing to hide the broad smile on his face. His age eluded her though.

"I'd very much like to get to know you. You look familiar to me and I don't know why. Have you been here before?" He sat down, placing one of the pints of ale in front of her.

"My daughter looks like me." She spoke softly overwhelmed by this man who seemed to be friendly yet Oscar had acted that way the first time she met him. She would have to be careful not to fall into the same trap.

"The McKenna's wife," he paused, looking toward the couple who were visiting with Alistair and Brenna. "You are the spittin' image of her." He grinned at her showing a wealth of white teeth behind the dark beard.

"She's my daughter," Heather said. "Until today I haven't seen her since I gave birth." Strangely, at the thought moisture didn't pool in her eyes.

Elliott held her hands in his. For a second, she thought to pull away from him, but they were calloused from hard work, warm and she felt protected by him. An emotion no man had ever elicited in her.

"May I ask your name?" He didn't let go of her hands, but his dark blue eyes sparkled as if amused.

Heather's heart raced while she struggled to drag air into her lungs. She tugged and he let go, still grinning as if he understood the strange affect his presence had on her. "Heather Duffy."

"Heather, 'tis a nice name. So, you are visiting or here to stay?" he asked, holding his mug before drinking deeply. "Try the ale. If you don't like it, I'll bring you a tankard of mulled wine."

"I hope I'm here to stay," she said, trying the ale and coughing. "I've never had ale before."

"So you prefer wine." He started to leave the table and Heather assumed it would be to fetch the wine.

She reached out to him, her hand shaking. "Never had wine either, but I like this. Don't leave." Someone brought a platter of food to the table where they sat. "I like your company."

He leaned back in the chair, seeming relaxed and at ease. His long well-muscled legs were stretched out in front of him. "Tell me more about yourself."

"Not much to tell. Why don't you talk about yourself instead? I'm sure that would be much more interesting."

"I'm a crofter on McKenna land. The first part of my life, one might have called me a wanderer. Never found anywhere I felt at home until I walked onto this land owned by clan Chattan. Don't know how much you *ken* about the McKenna's but I'm like them."

"How is that? What are they like?" She was curious now, looking over the people in the room then her gaze settling once more on Connal. There was something about the clan that was different, and this man said he was like them, different, unique perhaps. She wasn't, but her daughter seemed to have a tiny bit of that air about her.

"I'm not at liberty to say," Elliott said, his voice gruff, "but sometime if the McKenna comes to trust you, I'll show you. That is if you are here to stay. I certainly hope you are."

"I want to stay and I want Connal McKenna's trust, but more than that I need my daughter to trust me." On her journey to the northern highlands she'd thought a long time about her daughter and the reception, terrified she might be immediately rejected. Her welcome had been hesitant, but she could tell Wynnie wanted to reach out to her. Whether or not she would come to love her, remained to be seen.

She felt strange and apprehensive yet her thoughts flew back to the times when she was a young girl and dreamt of romantic love. How her thoughts ended up there she couldn't say. But this man was different and despite the years of abuse, she wanted to spend more time with him. Would like to feel the tender touch of a man's hand.

For a while, they ate in silence, simply because she had no idea what to say, and it didn't seem he wanted to talk either. He spent most of the time enjoying the food and laughing as he watched the room, his gaze always returning to her.

Then he stood and she was sure he would leave. "I'll show you around the castle if you like?" He extended a hand.

She was hesitant at first then remembered how secure she felt when his fingers closed around hers earlier in the day. "I think I'd like that. I know where my chambers are but not much else."

"If you'll go to the parapets with me, I'll show you my home. You can see it from the tower. Mayhap you'd like to visit me sometime."

Her knees were shaking. "Are we going to be alone?"

"Most likely. Do you have a problem with that?"

Then she blurted, her heart aching for something she'd never believed could come true. "I've never been alone with a man who didn't hurt me."

With her words she shocked him. His voice gruff and his eyes darkening, crease lines on his brow, "I would never harm you in anyway but if you don't want to go, I'll understand. We could walk where there are lots of people."

She laughed softly, amused, "Is there a place like that?"

"I was going to say the gardens, but this time of the day most likely we would find ourselves alone there also. What would you like, Heather? The choice is up to you."

She inhaled long and deep, believing this man could change her life for the better. Still, she could be wrong. She didn't have experience in deciphering the ways of men or their intentions, having known only one type of man.

Deciding courage should be her mantra, "To the parapets. I'd like to see where you live and the view of the countryside which I'm sure is spectacular." Her breaths were short and raspy and he grinned seeming to appreciate the affect he had on her body.

"If you like, we could ride there tomorrow, to my home."

She stopped midstride. Then, knowing she had to tell this man everything, "I haven't ridden since I was fifteen," *and my life changed for the worst.*

"Why is that?" his voice sounded concerned. "Why would you stop doing something that is so enjoyable?"

Once again, she inhaled a deep breath holding it for a few seconds before slowly letting it out. Then in a soft whisper, "Because I was held prisoner by a horrible man." She felt his fist tighten around her hand and she sensed he was angry but not at her.

"This is the man who hurt you." His voice was deep and gravely sounding.

"Yes, and others. You see, he sold me to his friends." He would not want to take that walk, would most likely not want anything more to do with her.

He stopped, turning to face her then lifting her chin, she looked into what seemed to be compelling and gentle eyes, "I would endeavor to change your impressions of men, but you have to learn to have confidence in me and *ken* that I would never do anything to cause you pain. Can you do that, lass?"

She was nodding her head, wishing she could form the words to tell him that for a reason she didn't understand she did trust him.

"I need to hear the one word."

She was still nodding, her body shaking. Then, "Yes. I want that, would like to trust someone."

"Good then, we'll proceed slowly." He offered his arm, which she accepted. "To the parapets."

Chapter Six

Spring rolled onto the Scottish countryside with elements of both rain and sunshine. It seemed everyday had a little of both. Brenna was with child now and Alistair seemed to dote on her, racing around the keep, trying to second-guess what she wanted or craved. She would reprimand him, telling her husband she was perfectly capable doing things for herself and that she wasn't an invalid.

Somehow the days between December and March got away from them and now the marriage of the two was planned for the next day. The clan had come in from the hills to celebrate the previous wedding of their laird as well as the upcoming nuptials of his sister and best friend. The cooks were busy in the kitchen creating all types of delicacies for the rest of the day as well as the feasting for the wedding day. Ale and wine flowed.

Connal stood with Wynnie on the parapets, his arm around her watching the road leading to the castle. He was always alert for incoming visitors, especially Oscar and Perkins.

"Are you happy, lass?" He turned toward her studying her profile before she shifted her full attention toward him. Her smile didn't seem sincere and he feared she thought along the same lines as he did. Their lives would be so much easier when they knew neither Oscar nor Perkins would arrive unannounced.

"Yes, and no," She touched his cheek with the palm of her hand, a tiny smile on her face. "Do you wonder when Oscar and Perkins are going to show up and if they do show up, I think Heather should stay in the castle instead of with Elliott as she has been doing. Oscar will want revenge when he discovers how happy she is and that she is wed to a good strong man. He resents everyone and what they have even if it's as simple as joy."

"I'm praying he's lost interest in both of you." He turned his face toward her hand, kissing the palm. Trying to figure out some way to draw the two men to the McKenna land so they would arrive on his terms and when he was prepared to meet them.

She gasped at his touch. He grinned realizing months ago he would never grow tired of this woman and the way the smallest caress affected him. She was his moon and his stars as well as the source of all the sunshine in his life.

"But you don't think he has given up."

"I would be surprised if Oscar quit. He thinks of you as his possession. Perkins on the other hand seems to be easily diverted by anyone wearing a skirt." His hands bracketed her waist as he held her close. Wishing they were alone in the bedchamber, he softly brushed her lips with his once then twice.

When he looked at her again, her mouth was damp, the moisture left from the caress shimmering in the muted sunlight of the vanishing afternoon. He brushed his thumb across her soft full lips, delighting in the slight trembling of her body and the small noise from the back of her throat. He would never stop wanting and needing her.

"We should go downstairs. There is still much to be done before the wedding. Brenna, although the two of them have been handfasted since October, is a bundle of nerves. She's a mess. Every time I bring up something that needs to be done, she has this strange high-pitched laugh."

"What is it you need to do?" Connal asked, wondering why the women folk were so busy.

"To begin with, the finishing touches on her dress. Tomorrow morning we will have to pick the flowers. The cook will finish the cake in the morning then we will have to get Brenna ready for her soon to be legal husband, at least in the eyes of the British government."

"I see and all the men folk have to do is carry a basket of stones around the village until his soon to be bride takes pity on him and gives him a chaste kiss." Unable to help himself, he was chuckling softly, thankful he had not had that task presented to him.

"I suppose that's all besides showing up. Are you going to be Alistair's best man? If you are, I'm sure you will do a fine job making sure your sister does not run off before the nuptials."

Connal began to laugh harder realizing because of the haste of his marriage to Wynnie many traditions besides creeling were left undone. He pointed to the courtyard below, "Look, I say, Alistair is fortunate he only has to carry the creel around the courtyard instead of through the village too."

"Appears that someone filled it to the brim with stones. Even the mighty Alistair is staggering under its weight and having difficulty with the basket." Wynnie laughed at the site along with her husband. "Do you think Brenna will emerge any time soon to give him relief with a kiss?"

"I'm sure she plans on making him work a bit longer. See, she is over there watching for the right opportunity." Connal had turned Wynnie in his arms. She now leaned against his chest, his arm circling her just below her breasts, his hands slowly moving upward while she wriggled within his strong hold.

"And I'm sure admiring her *bonny* bridegroom while enjoying his kiss," Wynnie said. "I would that you..." she paused with a soft sigh, "Well, that is not to be." She waved a hand in the air. "Forget that."

"Would you like a real wedding? It could be arranged. I doubt if either Alistair or my sister would object to a double wedding tomorrow if I suggested something of that sort," Connal asked, refusing to forget anything. "I would give you everything you asked for if I had the power, a wedding is one of the simpler things."

"No, I never expected to have a life separate from Oscar and Perkins. Thought I would forever be at their mercy. I'm very lucky to have found you and would change nothing. A wedding is not something that I need to be happy. All I want is you."

"I'm glad of that, lass. I'm lucky to have found you also." He wondered if she loved him. True, she now understood he was her mate but did she love him?

She let out a long slow sigh, relaxing into him, her soft curves enticing him with wicked thoughts. They would have to put in an appearance to the festivities of the night but after that, he meant to spend the evening alone with his wife pleasuring her in any way she suggested. She would have to get up early to help with the bride, so he would have to put her to bed early.

"It seems Brenna doesn't have torture in mind for her new husband. She is already in his arms." Connal pointed below. "Should we join them? Looks as if your mother and Elliott are there also. We have much to talk about with them."

"Suppose we have no choice. Brenna will be disappointed if we don't show up and spend a few hours toasting the bride and groom."

"But Alistair would rather just proceed to the wedding bed. As would I," Connal said, trailing a line of kisses down her neck, enjoying the process even more when she lifted her chin giving him more access.

When they arrived below, it seemed the people of the clan were assembling for the celebrations, laughing and chatting, catching up with old friends and meeting new ones. Bagpipes played in the hall and the ale streamed non-stop. Connal held back no expenses for his sister's wedding. Now she was dancing with Alistair and he was twirling her around the main floor. There were tents outside with vendors selling their wares, beads, bobbles, cloth whatever a person might want. The wedding would be profitable for the surrounding merchants as well as most of the clan.

"Would you like to dance, lass?" Connal asked, hoping this time Wynnie would at least try.

She held back, her hands behind her anticipating him. "You know I've two left feet. No matter how hard I try, I trip and will probably bring you down with me."

"Well then, lass, you'd be on top of me and a slight roll..." He grinned wickedly, delighted with the slight blush on Wynnie's cheeks. "We will dance one dance. I promise you can step on my feet as much as it pleases you or is necessary for you to remain standing. I guarantee I will keep both of us upright."

She punched him on the chest and he laughed drawing her closer for a swift brush of his lips across hers. He felt her melt into him and was tempted to say goodbye for the moment to his clan and carry her upstairs to their bed. He held back though, beginning to dance with her, moving slowly at first before picking up speed. The bagpipes were lively. Their feet not so much.

From the last time she tried to dance she had improved. The tune lasted for a few more minutes, and he managed to dance with her until they reached the table where her mother and Elliott sat.

He pulled out a chair for her. "Thank you for the dance. Perhaps you would like to speak with Heather while I talk to her husband. There are some things we need to discuss. The pause will give time for you to catch your breath."

"If you insist," Wynnie laughed while she gulped air, sitting down and helping herself to the pint of ale that had been set in front of her while Elliott and Connal strode to a distant part of the room.

"They are going to guess what it is we are about," Elliott said, his attention riveted on his wife. "You're worried Oscar will show up here and Heather will tell me she has the right to know everything, will pester me until I divulge any current news so I'm not too sure what we are about, trying to keep secrets."

"Soon, I'm sure. The roads are passable and Oscar is a man who doesn't like to lose something he thinks is his." Connal's fingers tightened on his glass. "We need to figure out how to lure the two men here on our terms. I want to write the rules to the game that will play out as soon as they arrive."

"And the man believes both Wynnie and Heather are his." Elliott looked toward his wife, his fists tightening an eyebrow arching as he seemed to think. "I won't let him near her."

"For Heather's safety, you need to come into the castle until Oscar shows himself." Connal didn't really believe Elliott would agree to this but there was no other recourse.

Elliott lifted broad shoulders a look of chagrin on his face. "Could be all summer. Don't know when the man will make an appearance if he ever will. I've got crops to take care of and a growing family to feed. Don't think I can do that, run from a man who is less than a man. You well *ken* it is not my nature to flee from trouble."

"Couldn't help but overhear," Alistair slapped Elliott on the shoulder. "Sleep in the castle at night and work your land during the day. I'll help and I'm sure there are others who will lend a hand. Keep Heather here where she will not constantly be looking over her shoulder. She won't complain too much with her daughter close by."

"Appreciate the offer but still don't like waiting around for something to happen," Elliott said.

"We don't have to wait. Confronting Oscar in his home makes some sense to me too," Alistair said.

"True, but what if he's put this all behind him and doesn't want anything to do with either Heather or Wynnie?" Connal asked, still thinking to bring the man here. "No, he's going to come. The only question is when and I want his appearance here on our terms."

Elliott ran his hands through his hair clearly distraught. "Don't like what my gut's telling me. It's not good."

Connal remained quiet while the men spoke. "Going to Oscar's home is not an option, and I understand the reticence in waiting. Don't like to feel as if I'm always on the defense but that is what we are going to have to do. Both Heather and Wynnie believe Oscar will come for them. They also believe he will be here sooner than later."

"I'll agree to Heather staying inside the walls of the castle but I need to guard our home. She needs to be protected but..." Once again he ran both hands through his hair, "I can't stay here every night. I need to safeguard my land and my crops. Even with help from the clan, Oscar could still do something to ruin me."

"What does Heather want?" Connal asked, thinking Wynnie would have an opinion if he decided to leave her one place while he stayed at another. If given the choice, he was sure she would to choose to stay with him.

"She's not liking my reasoning although I must confess I haven't decided anything yet. Don't want to leave Heather alone even in the castle. Like to have her close by. That way I know what she is about and she is safe." Elliott sat down as a servant brought more drinks.

"Seems the women folk are talking. Think they are saying the same as us?" Connal asked as Wynnie turned her attention his way, motioning for him to join her and he assumed Alistair and Elliott as well.

"I'm sure Brenna has an opinion as does Wynnie," Alistair said, grinning. "Glad Brenna doesn't have anything to worry about unless Perkins comes along with Oscar. He had his gaze set on her last time. That's why we handfasted that night. Didn't want to make love to her unless there was some agreement between us. If she stayed in my room and my bed..." He didn't finish the sentence.

Connal knew what he stopped saying and he still, mate or not, didn't like the way Alistair went about seducing his sister. It wasn't well done of him. "You're right to not say anything more. While I *ken* it is far better you than Perkins seduce her that night, I still wish it had been done in a more proper or traditional way."

"But you would have done the same," Alistair said.

"Perhaps." Connal was unwilling to admit to that but if Wynnie had not been petrified that first night, he might have done the same and worried about the consequences later. Protecting her was all he could think about even then.

"So, nothing needs to be decided tonight. Both you and Heather will remain here through the revelry then you can make up your mind if you wish to return home," Alistair said.

"Don't know about the two of you, but I'm going to collect my wife. We need some time alone before chaos reigns tomorrow," Connal said as he headed toward Wynnie, thinking he would have an enjoyable night. Alistair and Elliott followed with the same intentions where their mates were concerned.

Connal stopped beside Wynnie, his gaze focused on her. "I've ordered wine and some of the delicacies the cooks have made for the rest of the evening to be sent to our room. I'd like to spend some time alone with my beautiful wife tonight, and I'm also going to pray nothing happens to tear me away from you." He extended his hand helping her to stand. Closing his eyes for a second, he enjoyed the moment and the small intimacy, knowing there would be more explorations this evening.

"I apologize for spending so much time away from you," she paused, "the wedding, you know." Then with a tiny lift to her shoulders, "Although it was you who insisted they have a big celebration. We've been working hard on Brenna's dress, but she continues to get larger." She leaned against his arm as they walked through the keep.

"Perhaps tonight we will make a little one," Connal said, wishing his wife was just as pregnant as her mother and Brenna. He couldn't help but wonder why not. Brenna had told him they were trying too hard but that didn't make a bit of sense to him.

They rarely spent a night apart and since December it had only been a handful of evenings when he didn't come to bed until early morning. Even some of those times, he would pull her into his arms and she would be more than warm and willing.

"I'm sorry," She pulled away from him, tears in her eyes. "I don't know what's wrong with me. I know you want children."

"*Ach*, lass, there is nothing wrong with you or me. God willing we will have many children, as many as you want. Once everything settles down around us and we know we'll never see Oscar or Perkins again, perhaps then you will conceive," Connal tried to reassure her as well as himself. He knew of couples who never had children, and he did pray they would not be one of them. She had a child a long time ago when she was very young but she lost the babe. He didn't think that was the cause but he didn't really know. Wynnie was his mate. He would support and encourage her through any of their trials.

"I have been nervous particularly as spring grew closer," she admitted. "I never want to see those two men again, but I understand you need to make sure there is an end."

He opened the door to their room. Just as he ordered, a fire had been built up in the fireplace, candles lit around the room and an enormous array of food and drink sat on a platter on a table near the bed.

He poured them both a glass of wine, "Where would you like to sit?" His gaze was focused on the big bed. When she looked that way, she shook her head. "There will be time enough to explore the possibilities there. For now," she paused, "I just want to relax in your arms."

"What's on your mind, lass?" he asked, lounging back and trying to make himself comfortable when all he needed was his wife as well as the closeness he always felt when she was near.

"My mother, she doesn't think Elliott will run from Oscar. She says she won't leave him even to remain safe herself." Wynnie plucked at her skirt and Connal understood her nervousness. He needed to vanquish her fears yet he didn't know how.

"You're worried about Heather. I ken it but she is an adult as is Elliott. They will make decisions based on their needs not ours. You will have to trust in her choices. She spent too many years by herself, alone, and now that she has found her soul mate..." He shrugged, understanding, "She will not want to leave."

Wynnie inhaled a long deep breath of air. "He will kill her as he will me if given the chance. He has men who will follow him here just on the assumption they will be given the spoils of what is left over after he has had his fun."

"You believe he will come with men?" Connal was surprised yet nothing about Oscar Adair should shock him. Oscar was a cunning man and would understand Wynnie and Heather. He paused thinking and Wynnie would be well guarded but with the element of surprise he might well take what he wanted.

"Come, lass." He held her close. "Alistair and I along with Elliott will figure someway to bring the two men to the keep. For the rest of the night, I want to make love to my beautiful wife."

~ * ~

With the rising of the sun Connal woke Wynnie with a gentle kiss to the cheek. She sighed softly, snuggling into him and wishing she had a few more hours to sleep but there was so much to accomplish this day, Brenna's wedding day.

She rose and was surprised to see that Connal had ordered a bath for her and set out clothes for her to wear. The dress was one she had never seen and it was beautiful.

"When did you purchase this?" she asked holding the gown up to her.

He showed a row of even white teeth even while he was slipping on his kilt. "I had it made for you as a special surprise for today. The plaid is the McKenna dress plaid. I wanted our people to know how much you mean to me and that no other can take your place."

"Thank you." She wasn't at all sure what to say. The two words seemed so small to express how she felt. She smiled, wishing she had something to give him.

"You're quite welcome. The gesture is for me too. I want to show you off to our clan and let everyone know how proud I am to have you on my arm and next to me for the rest of our lives," Connal said, his voice gruff with emotions.

He always lightened her mood, not that today needed any help. "In any case, you will have to help me dress. So don't go very far. This morning you will not be able to get out of the ladies' maid duty by sending Brenna to me as she will be preoccupied as well." Wynnie enjoyed the play of emotions on her husband's face. She pointed a finger at him then shaking it at him with a grin, "Don't you dare leave or I will make you regret it. Don't you dare get any ideas about undressing me instead."

"In case you haven't noticed, you are quite undressed right now. Well, you know my preferences. Not safe for me to stay if we want to get to our duties on time," he muttered.

"Go on then. I will have to fend for myself," she said in a huff, waving her hand towards the door.

"I could send Heather to help you," he said as he slipped into a white shirt then a dark blue, velvet jacket before fastening his sporran. "It won't be a problem. I'm sure your mother would be pleased to come to your aide."

With her hands on her hips, devoid of clothing, she turned to him, "You could but you would regret it. This is your job today and you're shirking it." With a huge sigh, perhaps they should give up and go back to bed.

"You cannot say *nay* to me as well you *ken*. If I wanted to seduce you right this instant, you would melt in my arms, a pool of mush at my feet, just for me to have my manly way with you." He laughed as he stepped toward her. The raw passion in his eyes told her she should stop enticing him and settle into the hot water.

"I will only be a few minutes. You can wait that long for me." She hummed while she bathed and watched as he sat across the room staring at her. Perhaps it would have been better if he left and sent her mother to the room to help since she was feeling the heat of his gaze, her body responding to the silent invitation.

"Don't know if this is a good idea." Suddenly, he was kneeling beside the tub soaping a sponge. The glint in his eyes told her it was not something they should pursue.

"Go on with you. I give up. Send my mother or anyone else who is suitable that you run across. I should have found a ladies' maid months ago as both you and Brenna suggested and we would not be in this predicament. *'Tis* all my fault. I'm sure of it. I will shoulder the blame."

He let out a heavy sigh but seemed to think what she suggested might be the best idea for everyone involved. Dropping the sponge into the liquid, he turned on a heel, but he didn't leave the room. He returned and stooped over the tub then holding her head between both hands, kissed her long and deep, his tongue finding entrance and seeming to devour her even as he wove a silken web of enchantment around her. Ribbons of heat swept through her. She changed her mind. Brenna could wait a few minutes. She met his tongue with hers, her hands sliding along his legs, discovering what was not beneath his kilt.

"Keep that in mind for tonight." Then he left as if nothing happened between them.

She heard his laughter and understood she'd been outmaneuvered just now. Closing her eyes, she inhaled long and deep feeling the need for her husband and his arms around her. She quickly finished the bath and was able to dry her hair before Heather knocked on her door. Wrapped in a towel, she stood and welcomed her mother with a quick hug.

"Connal told me he wasn't up to dressing you this morning." She waltzed into the room. "And I can see why. Even if I say so myself you are a *verra* beautiful woman. You would be quite difficult to resist for any man and your husband, well, it seems he can never resist your charms." She stopped suddenly. "I'm sorry, the words were meant only as a compliment not a reminder of times best forgotten."

"Thank you, I didn't take your words that way, but you wouldn't be prejudiced or anything, now would you?" Wynnie asked, her laughter light and infectious. She laughed some more.

Her mother started to laugh too, "Of course I am prejudiced. Now, let's see how quickly we can get you dressed in all this Scottish finery and into Brenna's room to help her out. She already has several of her friends there. They are washing her feet. I was never really sure why that tradition evolved unless some groom thought his new wife's feet were dirty and suggested to others that her feet should get washed before the ceremony and the bedding."

"I'm sure you are right. Dirty feet would be horrible in bed."

"Just hold still so we can get this done properly," Heather said, a beautiful smile on her face.

Wynnie was standing as Heather brought her one garment after the other and helped her with the fastenings. "Now, you understand that when Oscar comes you should not be staying at your husband's home. It is not safe. You must take care. We both know he will stop at nothing to get you back in his custody. I'm sure he is ruing the day he let you go."

Heather was pinning a broach, the luckenbooth that Connal had given her, on her shoulder. It was silver and engraved with two intertwined hearts topped with a crown.

"There, that is almost as beautiful as you," Heather said, gazing at her admiringly. "What I do understand is that where I decide to stay and what chances I'm willing to take are between Elliott and myself. I *ken* the danger though and am loathe to be taken back to my prison. Elliott will never let that occur and would join forces with the rest of the clan to keep that from happening to me, or you, for that matter."

Yet to Wynnie's ears her mother didn't sound too sure of herself.

"You must be terrified of seeing Oscar again. Of course it is between you and your husband, but what does Elliott want you to do. He couldn't possibly want you to stay with him, could he?"

Heather stepped back letting out a rush of air as her body visibly shook. "Needless to say, we don't agree on this but even though I'm loath to do his bidding, I remember Oscar and the numerous assaults over the years. I don't want to be in that position again, at his mercy. Does not sit well with me even though I don't want to leave my husband. Perhaps he let me go because I'm too old for him. He did always have a penchant for younger women, young girls to be exact. And yet," she paused, "he does not like to lose anything he deems as his."

"Perhaps in this you should do Elliott's bidding. Connal has reassured me that he will send a message that is sure to bring the two men to the castle within their time frame." Wynnie hoped it was true. She didn't want to spend the next months looking over her shoulder or always going to the battlements to peer down the road.

"What we should do is stop worrying and find Brenna. We need to enjoy the day. When I left, the servants were bringing in food and drink. Are you hungry?" Heather asked, stepping towards the door and seeming to want a change of subject.

She also needed for the conversation to go in a different direction. It was after all Brenna's wedding day. "Starving, Connal kept me up most of the night doing the most..." Wynnie stopped then putting her hand over her mouth. One just didn't speak to their mother of such things.

"As did Elliott with me. Our men are an incorrigible lot and when they are in bed, they have one thing in common as well as one thing on their mind. I've grown used to my husband's touch and the pleasure he gives to me."

"I'm not with child though," Wynnie touched her belly, pushing back the threatening tears. "It seems of the three of us, I'm the only one."

"You will be as soon as Perkins and Oscar are gone from our lives. It is the tension and the fears that keep you from conceiving," Heather said, her smile brightening the morning for Wynnie. "We just don't know what or when anything is going to happen."

"But you carry Elliott's *bairn*. Aren't you stressed too?" It was a puzzling question to Wynnie.

Heather reached with a small lift to her shoulders. "Women react in different ways to different situations. Of course I'm worried, but I've spent years more terrified than I am now. With every footstep outside my door, I found myself shaking in terror. Elliott gives me a reason to love and enjoy life. I try not to look to the past or the future. I'm living in the present and enjoying every second."

"I suppose I should feel the same but..."

"You're young and terrified of losing what you have. While I feel the same to some degree, I want to live each day loving my husband and enjoy his tenderness. While he is a huge and powerful man, I do believe he is the gentlest sole on this earth."

"I'm glad for you and perhaps I should feel the same. I did spend six long years under Oscar's power, but after the first few assaults I was able to escape. Father rarely found me. I usually hid deep in the woods in a small cave I found where I stashed blankets and fire wood for the long winter days and nights. Even when there were no men to pay for my body, I kept to myself in fear of my father who rarely let a day go by without giving me to someone."

"Come, let's not speak of the past when our futures are so promising." Heather stepped back. "I do believe you are perfect in every way. The gown will tell everyone how much you mean to your husband."

Arm and arm they strode through the hallways until they reached Brenna's room. As Heather predicted the women just finished washing Brenna's feet and one young lady found the ring in the small tub. Tradition said she would be the next to wed.

"We are finally here," Wynnie said as she was handed a glass of wine.

"And it's about time too," Brenna said laughing, as she waited for the next layer of clothing.

"I really need something to eat before I start drinking," Wynnie said, sipping the beverage and enjoying the taste even while her stomach growled its displeasure.

When finished, Brenna was dressed in the Stuart dress tartan. "Well, you are about to become a Stuart. Any reservations?" Heather asked. Once again, she was standing back and admiring the young woman in front of her.

"None at all," Brenna said, smoothing her skirts before accepting a glass of wine. "I've been his wife in every way since the end of October. This just makes everything that much more special."

"You should eat something," Wynnie said. "It's probably going to be a long day then Alistair will whisk you off to his chambers for a long night of lovemaking. You will need sustenance if you want to make it through the night."

"I believe he is going to whisk me off to his ship. We would like some time alone and away from everyone else. Since we can't leave McKenna land until all of this is finished with Oscar Adair and Perkins, we decided to spend some time on his ship even though it is not going anywhere. Connal assured me the cooks made sure we had plenty of food onboard."

Wynnie felt a bit of jealousy. She had spent no time away from the castle with her husband. This was something she didn't know about Alistair Stuart. She wondered if her husband owned a ship too.

"An entire fleet of them." Brenna seemed to guess the question before it was asked. "Well, the McKenna's have four ships. We mostly send goods to France in exchange for their fine French brandy, the wine and champagne as well. They like the wool from our sheep among other things. The trade has been quite lucrative for the clan."

"I see," Wynnie plucked at her skirts, feeling more than a little insecure and jealous as well, "Why wouldn't Connal tell me something like that?"

"It's no secret. You didn't ask and he didn't think about telling you. Men are like that, a bit obtuse. If they can't see a reason for you knowing something unless you ask, they usually don't bring it up," Brenna said. "In any case, if things get really bad with your father, Connal can take you for an extended voyage and a visit in Paris. Do you speak French?"

"A little," she said a bit distracted at the moment.

"Perhaps the two of you can go on a belated honeymoon when all this business with your father is finished."

"That would be nice but at the moment all I would relish is peace and quiet and the knowledge we will be left alone to live our lives without worrying about what might happen the next day or even the next second." Wynnie finished her wine. "Are you ready to say your vows?"

The women left the room, still chatting. Stepping outside, the sun was warm and if there had been clouds in the sky, they vanished. Alistair and Connal stood in front of the Kirk doors. They were both grinning and watching them as they approached. At least one hundred guests stood outside waiting for the bride to appear and the vows to be said.

For a moment Wynnie had a bout with jealousy again. Saying vows to Connal was important to her. Maybe she could find a time tonight to tell him how she felt and that she would pledge her life to him. She needed to tell him her personal vow and how she felt. The first wedding had been necessarily brief and held few if any tender moments to hang onto, as they grew older.

Wynnie was one of the bridesmaids in respect for her position as sister in law. Brenna had two others who were escorted by Fergus and Angus McKenna, cousins to Brenna.

When the vows were finished, they headed inside for the Nuptial communion and blessing of the food.

Wynnie now stood beside her husband, leaning into him as she watched the happy couple. There had been weddings where she grew up, but she only attended a few. Fear for her wellbeing always accompanied celebrations of any sort. Her father would give her to any man attending the festivities who voiced they might want her.

The revelers sent the happy couple off to the ship amidst a flurry of rice and ribald comments. Wynnie felt Connal's hand creeping higher on her ribcage and pushed it down, laughing.

"Not here. You *ken* I'll give you whatever you want in the privacy of our room. Don't you dare seduce me here and now."

"Then I believe we've come full circle. We spent the day at the wedding of my sister and best friend, now we shall spend the evening celebrating our life together."

He swooped her into his arms, twirling her around a couple of times before carrying her into the castle and up the steps to the battlement. Where he set her down, they could see Brenna and Alistair riding toward the sea.

He pulled her close, brushing his lips across hers, his hand cupping her breast, his thumb rubbing across her nipple. "That was nice but I'm an impatient man."

"Why did you bring me here then?"

"I believe this was the place of our first kiss." He smiled at her tenderly pushing hair from her face. "I didn't know it would happen at the time I first saw you, but you have changed my life for the better."

"I've put the castle at risk."

"You are my mate and I as well as the clan don't care about any danger you might have brought with you. We will defend you without hesitation. I don't know what it was but that first evening, I behaved badly. Did things I'm ashamed of. It didn't seem as I could help myself. To me you were ravishing, still are."

"Truth be told, I could have fought harder. I think I wanted you to catch me but would never admit it even to myself. I was furious you brought me to the tower room and sought to leave me there alone with the rats."

"It was only a ploy so you would willingly accept my chambers over the other possibilities. I wanted you from the moment I first saw you. I wasn't about to give you a chance to get away," Connal laughed, running his hands down her back. "Shall we move on to the master chamber and more pleasant endeavors?"

She could never refuse him. He was her eternal love.

~ * ~

Oscar read the message from Connal McKenna for the second time. Pacing the room, he realized the power now was not in his hands.

Connal threatened him subtly but nonetheless his words were a threat not a warning. He wanted to see him and Perkins by the end of the month.

This was not how he planned the next meeting with Wynnie and Heather. He didn't like the summons. Quickly, he penned a message to Perkins expecting the man to show up when he felt like it. Since Wynnie escaped him last October, Perkins spent little time here. Almost a year had passed and he believed the McKenna had forgotten.

He resumed his pacing, looking out the window from time to time and watching the rain slip from the sky. Leaving the room for any reason this time of year was abhorrent to him. His limbs ached when he rode in a carriage for too many hours. He liked his meals on time and served at his dinner table along with his French brandy afterwards. And, to replace Heather and Wynnie, he found two whores who actually enjoyed his proclivities of force or at least they put up with him for the money he paid. That fact bit at him. He would have to figure out a way to sell their services to his friends so he could reap the multiple rewards.

Oscar poured himself a brandy, setting the message to Perkins aside and planning on sending it in the morning. Ringing the bell on the end table, he waited for Summer Nectar to arrive. She was a much better lover than either Heather or Wynnie. She actually knew what to do with her body and didn't fade away into another world when he took her.

Closing his eyes, he waited for her, thinking of all the delightful things she would do with his man parts, things no one else had done. He must have fallen asleep because when he woke, Perkins was standing over him.

"When were you going to tell me?" Perkins asked, his voice shaking with venom.

Oscar sat up quickly, adjusting his breeches, "Tell you what?"

"That we were summoned to McKenna land. You realize it could be a trap." Perkins poured himself a drink, downed it in one gulp before pouring another.

"Of course I realize that and of course it's a trap. Where is Summer? I summoned her hours ago." He stood, striding to the door before looking out to see if she was in the hall. Perkins would have stopped her if he arrived before her.

"I sent her back to her room. Told her she could come back in an hour and she was to bring Autumn Rain with her. Right now we need to talk."

"About what?" Oscar drummed his fingers on the table. His impatience was eating at him. He wanted Summer and he didn't want to talk to Perkins about the McKenna summons. He just wanted it to go away.

"About what we are going to do," Perkins insisted, gazing out the window.

"And what would that be? We don't really have a choice now do we? The McKenna holds the upper hand and we will have to comply in some way, whether we like it or not."

"He just wants a truce between us and I, for one, am willing to agree to anything he suggests. I don't fight." He dusted off his waistcoat, pulling it down to cover his sagging belly. "So, if that is their wish, they'll be disappointed.

"No, and neither do I. The only fight I enjoy is one a woman will give me when we're having sex. Summer is perfect. She actually enjoys what we do. Never thought I'd find one woman like that let alone two."

"Don't delude yourself, both women like the money. If we'd paid Heather and Wynnie, they most likely would not have run off."

"You might have a point." Oscar was beginning to slur his words. He sat up straight, shaking his head to clear his vision. He didn't want to fall asleep before he could entertain Summer.

"You realize of course he wants to meet us at the Kinnel Stone Circle."

"Of course I do. What does it matter?"

"There are rumors about those stones," Perkins said.

"And what are those rumors?" Oscar had about as much as he wanted tonight from Perkins.

"People disappear there."

Chapter Seven

It was All Hallows' Eve. The slight breeze whispered of the evil coming their way. This year Connal knew the source of that evil. He shielded his eyes from the sunshine glinting off the mountains beyond, praying this would end soon. He and his men arrived at the circle of stones earlier than prearranged to make sure there were no surprises. The land was flat and one could see anyone coming at least a few miles across the grazing pasture before the hills rose high to break the view. It took all summer then into the fall before Perkins and Oscar would agree to his terms.

God, but he missed his wife. He kissed her goodbye two days ago, leaving her with strict instructions just in case Oscar decided to go to the castle instead of the Kinnel Stone Circle. He smiled, thinking of Wynnie, his *mo shiorghra*. The months away from her father changed her. When she first arrived, she was strong and resilient in some ways but also afraid of her shadow and terrified when anyone new visited. She didn't trust easily and seemed to jump at every sound. Now she was making friends and joining with the other women. Often, he found her head close with many of the clan, gossiping.

"You think they will come?" Alistair asked, leaning on his saddle horn, his brows furrowed together. "Not so sure myself. Why should they put themselves at risk doing our bidding?"

"We have what they want," Elliott said softly.

"They will be here. I didn't give them a choice. There are laws against raping women in Scotland. Exposure would put him in jail as well as create a scandal that would initiate more scandal. He would lose everything. While that scenario would give me pleasure, it would not give me as much satisfaction as watching the two of them disappear from my life forever."

"And you will persuade the pair the same way as you persuaded Maurina?" Angus asked while he looked across the grazing field. No roads led to this special place, just foraging animals, grass and some heather. The grass undulated in waves as the breeze sifted through the blades.

"It's a convincing argument. Life somewhere else, at least that's what we assume, or certain death." Connal stretched upward to see further, his fingers tense on the reins. While he gave the others and appearance of confidence and patience, he felt little of either.

"Whatever waits beyond those stones might be terrifying. I'm sure it is better than living in a British prison," Angus said.

"Anything is better," Fergus agreed with his brother. "Would never want to rot in prison. I'd take my chances with the unknown. Always did believe in the magic of life and all the possibilities. There are forces, natural and unnatural, out there that none of us can understand."

"It might be our word against theirs," Elliott offered, sitting up taller as if that might give him a better look into the distance.

"It would be except there is a certain British lieutenant whose daughter somehow found herself trapped with these two men. They forced her and took her virginity without her consent. The lieutenant has wanted revenge for some time now. It seems she has never been the same since it happened. Refuses to see people, especially men and keeps herself in her room."

"But he would have to be here," Alistair argued.

Connal nodded to the south. Three redcoats were riding toward them across the grazing land. "They will be here sooner than Wynnie's father and once intended."

"And Perkins and Oscar will be presented once more with the choice in front of them," Alistair said. "If they don't choose the stones, what then?"

"We fight to the death. They've also been told that was a choice,"

Connal said. "Told them if they didn't make an appearance we would find them."

"What if they walk into the circle and nothing happens?" Angus always the pessimist asked.

"Never happened before but if it does, then I suppose neither man will have a choice. They will be taken into custody if they refuse to fight," Connal said.

The soldiers drew closer and Connal was rewarded with the look of determination in the lieutenant's eyes. This would all turn out the way he expected.

"Where are the men?" he asked with noted impatience. "Thought you said they would be here."

"They will be." Connal spoke with an assurance he didn't' quiet feel. "In any case, they've been told we will hunt them down if they don't appear. Their fate will be much better if they come of their own accord."

"A buffer between them and me," the lieutenant agreed. "Personally, for what they did to my daughter, I'd string them up by their man parts if I had my way in this."

"Or castrate them," another soldier offered.

Connal thought either scenario would be fitting but if they lived through the ordeal, he and Wynnie would still find themselves looking over their shoulders. He didn't want that for her or her mother. No, the Kinnel stones were the answer that he hoped would please everyone involved.

"I prefer them to disappear. I don't ever need to wonder if they are lurking around some corner waiting for me, or if somehow they escaped the prison they were confined in," Connal said with a heavy sigh and apprehension. "My wife and her mother need to live in peace."

"Perkins has an eye for my wife too and I feel the same," Alistair said. "They either disappear or they die."

Elliott spoke up then. "Couldn't we castrate them before they walk through the stones to disappear? That way they won't be able to hurt another woman in any other place or time. People never change their true colors."

"That is a lovely thought," The lieutenant offered, sporting a broad grin. "Very appealing."

"We promised no violence if they came of their own accord. I'm a man of my word," Connal said, wishing he hadn't sworn such a thing. Castration would set some of his fears at bay.

"They wouldn't have come without the assurance," Alistair said, still searching the landscape.

"They still might not come. Don't see any indication of them yet," Elliott said seeming to search the horizon for any sign of people.

"It's still early," Connal spoke, realizing he had every confidence the pair would show up. "Patience."

The sun was nearly past its zenith when the two men were spotted riding toward them. Rain began spitting from the dark clouds that were scattered, giving an eerie feeling to the scene. It's a *dreich* day, fit for what we have to do here. Connal knew before the end of the day they would be soaked through to the skin and would need to take shelter for the night. They would not be able to ride home as planned until the next morning.

Perkins and Oscar stopped in front of Connal, grim expressions on their faces. They seemed to notice the lieutenant and his men. Their actions had finally gone full circle. They would indeed pay for their crimes.

"I see you came and I'm assuming a fight is not your first choice," Connal said, smiling inside for the first time since penning the letter to these two men.

"We would not win in that case," Perkins said speaking for both of them. "We are not fighters."

"No, you wouldn't but it would be against me and the lieutenant. The fight would be fair if you choose to reconsider," Connal said, understanding these two men needed to make the decision without being coerced.

"You must pay for your crimes against our women," the lieutenant spoke up, his voice harsh. "Me, I'd just as soon kill you or castrate you. It is what you deserve."

Oscar dismounted and walked toward the stones before he entered. He inhaled long and deep, looking backwards to Perkins expecting him to follow. "I've packed a satchel. I'm assuming I can take it with me."

Connal lifted his shoulders, "Take anything of yours you want."

He nodded, walking back to his horse then taking the reins into his hands. Only Oscar walked toward the circle and into the middle. In a blink he was seen then he was not.

At the sight a shiver snaked down Connal's spine. The same happened when Maurina walked into the circle of stones.

"Where did he go?" Perkins asked, his voice shaking as he started to turn his horse around.

"No you don't." The lieutenant and his men blocked Perkins.

Connal grinned, leaning on his saddle horn. "No one knows. You going to take your chances with the unknown or do you want to clash swords with the lieutenant here? If you kill the lieutenant, I will be next. For you there is no escaping your fate. You will die today if you make the choice to stand and fight."

Connal watched the man's Adam's apple bob up and down in his neck. He delighted in Perkins' fear. The man had never thought about the terror and pain he evoked with the women he forced. Castration as well as the walk through the Kinnel stones should have been the punishment.

"He would never vanquish me so... what is it you want?" the lieutenant asked. "Life or death?"

Perkins' finger ran around the collar of his shirt as if he tried to loosen it. "Suppose I'll take my chances in the circle of stones."

"You best hope you disappear," the lieutenant said.

"Or you'll follow me?" Perkins challenged.

"No, just wait until you get hungry enough to come out and meet your fate."

"Under the circumstances we've been more than generous with your lives," Alistair spoke up.

"Go on," Connal said, his grin wide now that he knew Perkins would vanish from this part of Scotland yet he prayed that wherever he showed up, he would be a wiser man.

"Very well," Perkins said then rode into the kinnel circle of stones and disappeared.

"Don't *hast ye back!*"

~ * ~

Wynnie smiled happily, knowing Connal was everything to her, her life, her mate through all eternity. Another year had passed since Oscar and Perkins vanished through the stones. Once more it was All Hallows' Eve. From the parapets they could see the bonfires on the horizon. It was their second year together.

Heather had been right. As soon as the tension and stress from knowing her father could show up any time vanished, she conceived. Now she sat in the solar, Connal beside her, watching her baby wave his arms excitedly in the air.

Brady was laughing and cooing at his father's antics. If Connal was *nay* careful, the baby would toss the contents of his stomach right in Connal's face. She laughed with them as Connal lay beside the infant, tickling his stomach.

"Do you think he'll be a shifter like you?" Wynnie asked, hoping the little boy would grow up to be just like his father.

"I think he will be," Connal spoke, still watching the child. "He has shown some subtle signs."

"Truly there was a time I didn't think I would have a child." She sat down on the floor next to her husband.

"I'm glad we have the babe, but it would not have mattered to me," he told her, holding his hand out to her suggesting she join him on the floor.

"And why is that?" She bent over and with her hands on either side of his head, kissed him, her tongue slipping over his lips in a silent quest.

"Because I'm a sucker for you, my darling Wynnie. You are my eternal love as well. Was the first time I saw you racing away from me in the darkness. I knew I had to find a way to make you mine."

"You didn't proceed as a gentleman." She pushed away from him, but he wouldn't have the distance. He pulled her on top of him as he lay back on the floor."

"Who's to say I didn't let you have your way because we will be together through eternity?" she asked, as he rolled over and was now bracing himself above her. His gaze was raw with breathtaking passion and her body seemed to melt beneath his.

"Don't you think it's time for Brady to take a nap?" he asked, kissing her softly across her collarbone then lower.

"He just woke," she told him, moving so he had better access to her neck while she arched toward him and he placed gentle kisses on her exposed skin.

"Where is the nanny?" He rose to look out the door then called out.

A woman appeared so quickly, she must have been waiting for the summons. Without direction, she seemed to know what to do and scooped Brady into her arms, leaving them alone.

Connal closed and bolted the door. Leaning against it he stared at her. "I'm thinking I'd like to see you with nothing on."

He began to undress, quickly slipping from his clothing then striding toward her. He was adept at women's clothing and despite the layers, she was suddenly naked beneath him.

"Should we work on a second child?" he asked as his lips explored her.

"I think we should wait until Brady is a bit older." She could barely breathe as his hands found all the magical and enchanting spots he knew so well.

"Don't know if I can do that." He slipped inside her, holding still. "But I'll try."

She ran her hands along his back. "How did I get so lucky to wander onto McKenna land?"

"Whit's fur ye'll no go by yet," she said softly.

"Yes, everything happens for a reason," he murmured as his lips found hers again and again. "God, I can't resist you. I'm such a sucker for you. Yes, you are my eternal love, Wynnie, my beloved, *mo shiorghra*. I love you, you know."

"I love you too," she murmured as she reveled in the magic and mystery that Connal so easily created in her. "All I ever wanted was to love and be loved."

"And so you are."

Coming Soon
by
Christine Young
at
Rogue Phoenix Press

In Brady's Arms

Chapter One

Scottish Highlands 1747

The last two years following the battle of Culloden had been turbulent ones. Connal McKenna as head of the clan Chattan somehow managed to maintain neutrality between the combatant Jacobites and the English. As a clan they united in choosing neither side. A few individuals chose to fight with the Jacobites, but there were not enough for the English to turn their hatred and vengeance against the entire clan. Still, the English patrolled the area searching for any man who might have fought against them.

Rumors abounded about a group of men who helped the wanted Jacobites escape Scotland to sail to America where they could live in relative freedom.

Brady McKenna, the oldest son of Connal and Wynnie, sat in a room adjoining the kitchen sipping a glass of ale. Relaxed and in his prime he searched for diversions. His gaze was focused through the doorway on a newcomer, her hands deep in bread dough, flour smudged on her cheeks and the tip of her nose. Her eyes were the clearest softest blue, her cheeks pink from exertion and the excessive heat of the kitchen. Her golden-reddish hair was piled high on top of her head, a scarf wrapped and tied to keep the strands from falling into her face. He wondered what her hair would look like, how it would feel against his naked flesh or if he threaded his fingers in the silken mass. She was tall for a woman, slender, almost too much to be attractive to Brady. Her pale gray dress did little to reveal but was adept at concealing what curves she might possess. The apron she wore, however, hinted of a tiny waist. Still there was a certain striking quality surrounding her, a haughty air that belied her status as a serving wench.

She was a puzzle to be figured out, he decided.

Until recently the clan accepted newcomers into their midst on a trial basis. Now, after the battle that left much of Scotland impoverished, Connal, the laird, was reluctant to even allow a wide-eyed innocent lass to gain access to the castle and the lands. So, how did she manage to secure a position inside the security of the castle walls no less?

Robby, his brother, sat down beside him, a grin on his starkly handsome face. His dark hair too long, he swiped away several strands that had fallen into his eyes. With a nod he began, "You seem distant. What's got you staring into the kitchen with that look on your face? It appears you mean to devour that sweet lass. She looks to be a tender morsel, too innocent for you or me for that matter."

"What look?" Brady grinned, lowering his lashes in an attempt to keep at least a few of his seething emotions private.

"That besotted expression you always get when you've seen a new conquest. Doubt if the lady stands a chance against you when you've set your sights on her," Robby said following the line of Brady's sight. Then with a bland tone belying the light in his gray eyes, "She doesn't look like one of your normal ladies."

"And what would that be?" Brady's voice was flat as the thought that Robby was right in his assessment. Nor, at this moment was she readily available. His father frowned on dalliances with the hired help. Discretion would be the word if he decided to pursue the woman. Ah, but if he first installed her as his mistress then his father would have no problems with what would be a short-lived infatuation.

"Well," Robby leaned back, stretching his legs out, one arm negligently propped on the chair next to him, looking much the same as his older brother, thoughtfully stroking his chin, "short, lots of curves and blond."

A frown marred Brady's face, his eyes narrowing as he looked at the chit again. Hell, she was nothing like the women he usually preferred. So, what was it about her that drew his interest? Fascinated him? He grinned when she made a face, her nose crinkling, her lips parting slightly.

She turned her head just then, sneezing. Most likely from the flour on the end of her nose. With the back of her hand, she wiped her forehead, more flour arrived on her tiny, perfectly shaped face.

He chuckled, amused by the scene.

"What's her name? Do you ken it?" Brady asked, turning to his brother in an attempt to put the lady out of his sight if not out of his mind at least until he discovered more about her. It wouldn't do for him to claim his feelings just yet.

"You really that interested?" Robby sounded surprised then in an ordinary tone. "Lillian Townsend."

"Sassenach."

"True, still she is striking in looks; too bad she is English. Father told me she's living in the Fraser cottage." At his quick look of surprise and a shrug of his shoulders, "She says she's a Fraser? The family hasn't been around in years. Heard tell one of them fought for the Jacobites. Father wouldn't want any of the clan settling into this area. Only bring trouble. So, what do you think he is doing?"

"She's lying." Brady was suddenly determined to discover what else the lady was not saying. Even though she intrigued and captivated him, he didn't trust her. Lust was never a reason to put oneself in danger. There was something else going on here. By the way she kneaded the dough, she didn't ken how to do it.

"Suppose she probably is," Robby agreed with a smirk on his face. "Suppose you're going to make it your mission to find out what she hasn't told the laird. This should be entertaining to watch."

"That is a distinct possibility." Brady rose from the table. Without looking back his long strides took him outside the castle walls. Curiosity driving him, he headed in the direction of the Fraser cottage eager to add to his knowledge about Miss Lillian Townsend. No one had lived there for almost fifteen years. The place should be rundown and dirty, uninhabitable. If she was destitute and had to work in the kitchen, why wouldn't she live within the castle where it was safer? There were rooms available for the servants. A woman shouldn't be alone, shouldn't be walking the narrow dark paths at night. His fists clenched.

Fifteen minutes later he strolled around the small home, stroking his chin as different thoughts filled his head. First, he walked the perimeter then knocked on the door. A polite reflex, he chuckled since she was at work. When no one answered, he pushed open the unlocked door, discovering the door had no lock. Neither did it have a bar to place over the opening to keep unwanted intruders from entering when she was at home, presumably alone.

Blood pounding furiously at her ignorance or nonchalance about her safety for a few seconds he stared around the room. The Frasers must have left everything behind when they moved. The place was clean, the furniture old and worn. He strode into the kitchen, opening cupboards and drawers to find utensils, plates and cups for two.

For two people? Robby said nothing about a second person. His annoyance as well as his curiosity blindsided him.

A broom. She had a broom. Well, the floor was clean and tidy.

He strolled into the bedroom. There was a large bed with warm quilts and pillows. The sight caused carnal thoughts to flow through his head. When he closed his eyes he could see her, entangled within his arms, her thick hair flowing down her back, wrapped sinuously around him. In the far corner a massive trunk sat. When he lifted the lid, he saw it was filled with gowns. Gowns in silk, satin and velvet. He delved deeper. There were all sorts of frilly frothy underclothing, corsets too. When he stared at her earlier, he would have sworn she wore only a chemise beneath her worn and very serviceable gray gown.

He sat on the bed, running his hands through his hair, thinking, wondering at what he discovered.

Still deep in thought, Brady wandered back to the main room. In the fireplace a stew simmered in a huge pot. Picking up a ladle, he stirred and tasted, examined the meat. Rabbit. When the hell did she have time to hunt and snare food to eat?

Obviously, she wasn't alone. A husband? A lover? His gut clenched at the thought of another man sharing her life.

A month earlier about ten red coats rode through here, searching. It seemed they never quit looking for Jacobites. They found no one. Brady knew there were rumors though, gossip that a handful of traitors were living near here in the woods. The last thing his family wanted were English soldiers traipsing over their land, enslaving people of the clan, discovering just how different they were. If that happened there would be no privacy, no way to shift and run wild over the heather throughout the ragged hills and cliffs. They would all be prisoners within their homes.

He was shaking his head as he turned toward the castle when a movement caught his eye. Stopping, he waited holding his breath, sensing that whoever he thought he saw was doing the same.

For a moment his breath caught in his throat his heart stopping. "Robby."

His brother grinned at him. "Thought I'd keep you out of trouble. Didn't like the way you looked when you headed out the door. Sure does look deserted doesn't it? What did you discover?"

"Thought you'd never ask," Brady said dryly, watching, hoping he would find the second person in this scenario. Wishing there was no one else. From what he'd seen of her so far, her entire life was a lie.

"Well, you don't have be sarcastic." Robby stuck his hands in the pockets of his jacket as he fell into stride beside him.

"Lillian does not live here by herself. She has a man with her if the rabbit simmering in the pot is any indication."

"Nay, you've got that piece of information wrong. Heard father saying he sent her the rabbit with his blessings and would help her with food until she was able to fend for herself."

Brady wasn't sure why he felt a small lift to his heart. He didn't like to think of her sleeping with someone or hiding someone either. The only person she was going to sleep with in the near future was him. If she was hiding someone, when caught the soldiers would imprison her just as quickly calling her a traitor as they would a man. Even though she was English through and through, they wouldn't care. They meant to make sure the rebellion was completely squashed.

By the time he reached the kitchen again, she was nowhere to be seen. It was just as well. His emotions were in turmoil. He wasn't at all sure what he would say to her when he did get the chance to speak with her and he would. There was no question in his mind that he would talk to her, the only question was when.

When he walked into the main room, his uncle Alistair was with his father deep in discussion. He sat down beside them, listening. Much of their conversation was the same. Now their conversations were always about when they would have their first grandson or daughter. Who would be first? None of their children were married yet. Not even his sister who was of age. Problem was she needed to find her mate. Perhaps their father should send her to Glasgow or Edinburgh for a period.

Brady sat next to his father, unwilling to waste time listening to their idle chat. He blurted, impolitely interrupting, "What do you know about Lillian Townsend? Why is she here?"

Connal slowly turned his gaze to his oldest son, his brows drawn together, clearly displeased with the untimely interruption. "I don't believe that is any of your business, son. Unless she wishes to say anything it is not my place to tell tales. I gave her permission to live in the Fraser cottage for as long as she needs to do so."

Brady heard the ice in his father's voice, giving him even more reason to seek out Lillian's truths as well as her lies. She was purposely hiding something from the laird, putting everyone in danger.

"Come, let's eat." Together they walked to the table designated for the laird and his family. Wynnie was nearly finished with her meal. Brady didn't believe he should engage his mother in questions about the woman who seemed to be occupying his head. She would see right through him.

He found himself leaning back in his chair, staring at the opposite end of the room. The food was unappealing tonight. He found he wanted to sample a bit of the rabbit stew with Lillian in her cottage.

"Is there something wrong with the food?"

The sweet sultry voice next to him shook him out of his melancholy musings. He looked up into the soft blue eyes he noticed earlier. She smelled of vanilla. He reached up and swiped away the flour on her nose.

She inhaled a sharp breath, stepping back so quickly she lost her balance for a moment. Brady reached out, stopping her fall. "My apologies. I only meant to rid your nose of the flour left from your baking today," he said with mocking disdain, still wondering about her as well as her intentions. "You don't ken much about cooking, do you?"

Lillian touched her nose, staring at him as if she thought he'd lost his mind. She was a skittish little thing, almost as if she wasn't used to men. He decided she was a good little actress. She had the emotions correct right down to the hand at her throat and the widening of her eyes, a deceitful little thing. Amused he slanted her a mocking grin. Unraveling her would be interesting.

"You had no right to touch me," she blurted suddenly, her eyes fixed on Robby as if she couldn't bear to look at him or she saw something she disliked.

"I was just trying to help," he growled, his gaze riveted on his brother who was grinning, clearly enjoying this encounter. His brother knew how he felt about the girl and was using this opportunity to mock him.

"Then I beg of you, don't help again. I'm quite capable of getting the flour dust off my own nose." She stuck her chin in the air. The regal tilt, the stiffness of her shoulders spoke of nobility.

Not a common serving wench. His thoughts returned to the silks and satins he saw in the trunk.

Another piece of the puzzle that was Lillian Townsend.

Then she cleared her throat, looked at him with an imperious glare in those soft blue eyes, repeating her earlier question. "Is there anything I can get for you, sir?" she stood back, waiting.

He reached out, confronting her earlier statement that he had no right to touch her as he placed his hand around her wrist, closing over her wrist, tugging her closer. "I want you," he said, his voice assuming a husky gentle timber.

The gasp of air, the sucked in breath was another good ploy. "Food, drink anything of that nature." She tugged on her wrist, seeming to ignore his statement. She would not ignore him forever.

"Tonight, when you are through working. Wait for me in the kitchen. I'll walk you home. Shouldn't be out there by yourself in the dark. 'Tis not safe for a pretty lady." He knew she would not, at least he knew she would try to leave without him seeing her. She would not succeed.

"No."

"Yes, I believe you will. We've matters to talk over. You can't deceive me like you have my father." He watched her eyes narrow. The soft blue turned to silver ice as she stared at him, never turning her gaze from his. She provoked him.

"I've not deceived anyone." She tugged again, her lips thinning into a straight line.

This time he let her go, hearing Robby clear his throat behind him. Something else was happening in the hall. His guess was that he had the attention of his father. "Tonight. That's a promise."

Without confirming his request, she fled the room, her skirts swaying gracefully around her feet her back stiff as a board. He placed his hands on his belly, watching, anticipating what was yet to come. He meant to discover her secrets as well as enjoy anything else that might come from their association.

"You're playing with fire, big brother. If father discovers what you're about, he'll be displeased."

Connal sat down, his hands folded on the table. "She is not what she seems. For your own good, leave her be."

In a dry tone, "I've figured that out by myself. This has nothing to do with my own good, rather hers."

"You should leave her be. She is not your mate." There was a tinge of anger in Connal's voice.

"It seems, I can't leave her be," Brady said in all honesty, his voice cold and hard, wondering why he felt so intensely when it came to Lillian Townsend. He thought on his father's words. 'She is not your mate.' How the bloody hell did one know if a woman was his mate? Ah, he brushed the thought aside. If he had to wonder, she most assuredly was not his throughout all eternity.

Thinking about that he decided it would not be unpleasant to have her for a few months.

She walked back into the hall, a tray of drinks and food in her hands. She was graceful when she moved. He liked everything about her except the deception and the lies. Lillian would be his, at least until he grew tired of her. He would begin the subtle coaxing he was known for this very evening when he accompanied her home.

He turned to his father, "Did you snare a rabbit for her?"

His question seemed to surprise Connal. "What if I did?"

Brady lifted his shoulders in a slow dramatic shrug, more questions coming to mind. "Something you don't do for the crofters. Is she more than just a tenant on McKenna land? Is she really a Fraser?"

"Leave it be," the laird said harshly, rising. He held out his hand for his wife. Together they exited the room, Wynnie looking over her shoulder, her eyes seeming to plead with him to do as his father asked.

He could not.

Normally, he would have given in to his father's wishes in a heartbeat. Something about this woman stirred his senses, provoking every masculine part of him; intrigued, fascinated, leaving him spellbound and needing more. He sought to kiss her senseless, possess her soft lips until she told him everything he wanted to know, until she gave him all of herself.

"I cannot," he whispered as Lillian whirled passed him another tray in her hand. The breath he inhaled was long and deep. The scent of vanilla floated around her. "God help me, but I cannot."

The seconds and minutes seemed to tick by more slowly than they ever had in his entire life. The great hall slowly began to empty. The servers were few and far between. When he watched Lillian slide passed him into the kitchen, he rose, following behind her.

Brady leaned against the doorjamb, arms crossed in front of him as he watched Lillian go through the process of leaving. If she realized he was there, she gave no indication as she wrapped her threadbare cloak around her. When she became his, he would make sure she dressed in the silks and satins she already owned, no more pretense. What she presented here was a complete fabrication of her life.

As she left, the room he pushed away, stepping at her pace until she was out the door. The darkness seemed to swallow her whole. Under his breath he cursed, wondering how many times she made the fifteen-minute walk to the cottage she was calling home alone by herself.

Anger simmered, annoyance at her flagrant abuse of her life flared deep in his soul. Did she truly think it safe for her to walk that distance by herself? After tonight, no longer would she put herself at risk. This was untenable. Furious strides ate up the ground between them until she noticed he was behind her.

"I told you to wait for me." His voice was cold with rage. He held on to her arm, turning her to look at him, needing to tell her that she would obey his commands.

She tried to wrench her elbow from him, her eyes darkening with her own anger as she stared at him, realizing she was helpless to resist. "I don't take orders from you, sir. Unhand me," she grit out between clenched teeth, her resentment with him simmering as hotly as his own.

"No?"

"No!" She swung at him.

He wasn't expecting her to retaliate. She moved like lightning. Her hand connected with his face so hard his head jerked back. He felt the fire on his face where she slapped him. He could even feel the imprint of her fingers forming on his cheek. Awe at her audacity filled him. Irritation at her inability to see the danger in the situation gave new meaning to his need to see this through to whatever end awaited them.

"You are an audacious piece of baggage." He held both her hands, tugging them behind her back, bringing her against him, her breasts pushing against his chest. He heard each breath as she labored to draw in air, felt the heat of her body pressed so near to his, felt the lush curves he had not seen beneath her serviceable gown. She lowered her lashes, another ploy he thought to get the better of him. If anything, she was a consummate actress.

Then she looked up. "Bastard!" she spat out. "Let me go."

His smile hinted at mocking amusement. "You, madam, are in no position to make demands. Perhaps it would be more prudent on your part to yield to my requests and humor me." He changed tactics. Request seemed much more biddable than the words demand or command.

"Jackal! Swine!"

"Sassenach." He spoke plainly.

She turned her head, seeming to school her features. "I'm a Fraser."

"Townsend."

He released her elbow. She continued walking as if he didn't match her step for step. The silence permeated his thoughts, soaking into every pore of his body. Her back was stiff, her strides long for a woman while her fists were clenched tightly at her sides. An apparition of frustration and fury, if he didn't miss his guess.

If she were a man, she would be a worthy opponent. As a woman, she would fall nicely into his plans. He was confident to believe all he needed to do to make her his was meet her lips with his own.

Soon.

Rain began to fall, a few drops at first then turning into a deluge with gusting winds. She pulled the hood of her cloak over her head, pretending he wasn't there or perhaps hoping he would disappear. He was sure the hood would blind her to him. A grin nestled in his heart sending signals of delight all the way to his toes. He didn't want to but he appreciated her stubborn infuriating courage. Still, she sought to win this game she was playing with him. Not by ignoring him she wouldn't.

A deer bounded across the path. She cried out, turning to him before realizing what she was doing. He pulled her close.

"'Tis nothing to be afraid of this time, Lilly. Next time the animal might be of human form," he murmured, his breath touching her face, his knuckles tenderly stroking her cheek. "Much more dangerous."

Placing both hands on his chest, she pushed on him. He didn't move as he turned her. When she looked up, his mouth was so close to her own, he could feel her rapid breaths against his lips. He watched her small tongue run across her full bottom lip that he knew would be soft and wet for him when he chose to kiss her.

"I'm not afraid."

"You must have been since you sought me out." His words were spoken with a bland indifference.

"I was just surprised. A deer nothing more or less. No harm." Her words were staccato like spoken quickly as if she still was robbed of air.

"Could have been a man. Someone who wished you harm," he said softly. "I would not have liked that."

"You wish to do me harm."

"Nay, I only wish to give you pleasure." *As soon as you will allow it.*

"I don't know what you're saying." She pointed down the trail where they were headed. "See, there is my home. You can leave now. You've seen me to my destination, and I thank you to go now."

"Not until I'm ready and I know there is no one dangerous inside waiting for you."

~ * ~

Earlier that afternoon, Lilly felt his insistent gaze before she saw him. When she turned her attention his way, he was sitting, his long well-muscled legs stretched out in front of him, one arm nonchalantly draped over a second chair. His eyes were the color of molten steel, his hair black as coal. The angles and planes of his face were hard and chiseled. Nay, all his body was hard, unyielding. Even sitting he was the personification of masculine grace. There was not one part of him that appeared soft. Every part of him oozed male confidence.

In one hand he held a glass of ale. His gaze riveted on her, on her lips, her breasts even as the focus of his attentions roamed down her body assessing her. In London she'd known men who were so arrogant they believed they had the God given right to anything or anyone they desired. This man appeared to be cut from the same ilk. Though he made no move toward her. A sudden unexplainable wave of fire swept through her.

Not yet.

In part that was why she fled the horrid country as well as the more horrific town, littered with vices of every kind. Every nobleman kept a mistress or made use of the whores who dotted the waterfront taverns. Few were loyal to their wives and visa versa. The stink of the town filled her with dread as well as revulsion. Even more so was the knowledge her father promised her to a man three times her age. She could not stomach the notion of lying in bed with the vile creature and allowing him to do what he wanted with her body.

Her gaze returned to the man staring at her, joined by his brother. She knew who they were, recognized the McKenna brothers by the steely purpose of their long strides and broad shoulders. They possessed the same hard gray eyes as their father. The laird warned her to stay away from his sons when he allowed her to reside in the Fraser cottage. Not because he didn't deem her worthy of knowing her sons but to keep her from getting hurt. They would only wed their mate, she understood. They loved women and never said no to a willing lady or one they could coax into their bed. Every unwed woman was fair game if they wanted a dalliance.

A woman had hurt Brady a few years back. Believing her his soul mate, he fell in love with her, offering her a place by his side through eternity, offering her everything he was. Later he discovered all she wanted was his title and wealth. The lady was no more his mate than she was. She was here with a purpose, one she meant to fulfill. She would never allow a man such as Brady McKenna to dissuade her from her good and true purpose.

Inwardly Lilly laughed. It seemed it was true of all women, even those living in the highlands. Until now, she thought it a trait of the women in London seeking to better themselves. Well, she didn't have the time or the inclination to form a relationship with anyone, let alone one of the brothers, especially not Brady McKenna. She wiped her hands on her apron, finishing with the bread dough, allowing a heavy sigh to escape her lips. It wasn't as if she disliked the work. She dreaded it because she was so bad at it. The kitchen had never been her domain. No, she was more accustomed to the parlors and sitting rooms in the elegant townhouses of the London affluent, to being served not serve.

As the evening wore on and she'd been given the ultimatum that Brady would walk her home, she dreaded the upcoming moment. She wasn't afraid of him. When he touched her, held her wrist with his long slightly calloused fingers, she knew she was afraid of her feelings for him. He wasn't gentle by any means, but she sensed he could be, suspected he could melt her heart as well as her body if given the opportunity. If she could only escape out the back door before he had a chance to know she left, she would be able to breathe a little more freely. Perhaps her heart would even stop thundering so harshly beneath her ribs. She would not have to worry that he would discover what she was about here in the highlands.

She understood the chance of escaping him was slim. He was a determined man. Had not been surprised when she spotted him leaning negligently against the doorjamb into the kitchen when she was ready to leave. She braced herself for the confrontation as well as his presence beside her while he escorted her home. She prayed her brother, Douglas, would hear them and leave the crofters hut just in case he insisted on seeing her inside. He needed to remain hidden and unobtrusive for the next few weeks so he could heal then resume their mission.

The rain began to fall, a few drops at first before turning into a deluge with gusting winds. She pulled the hood of her cloak over her head, pretending he wasn't there or perhaps more to the point wishing he would disappear. She quickened her pace, hoping to reach the cottage before she was drenched to the bone. His presence beside her unnerved her, completely terrified her. A lump caught in her throat. Her knees quaked so hard she could barely place one step in front of the other. Maybe if she stepped inside the door then slammed it shut in his face, he would understand she didn't want him to come inside.

Perhaps the world would stop turning.

A deer bounded across the path. "Oh!" she cried out, turning to him before realizing what she was doing. He pulled her close. His arms wrapped around her, warm and hard, inflexible, demanding. She had naught to give.

"'Tis nothing to be afraid of this time, Lilly Townsend. Next time the animal might be of human form," he murmured, his breath touching her face, his knuckles tenderly stroking her cheek. "Much more dangerous."

In her heart, she understood he was the most dangerous animal she would encounter.

Placing both hands on his chest, she pushed on him. He didn't move as he turned her. When she looked up, his mouth was so close to her own, intimidating, yet strangely beckoning to her. Her lips parted. She moistened them with her tongue as she struggled against her fears as well as her escalating emotions. This was not something she was accustomed to. She had never been held so close, so intimately by anyone. While she danced and was held by other men, the sensations were never like this. The threat of his hard body pressed against hers caused a strange ache as well as heat to gather inside.

"I'm not afraid." She tried to swallow, tried to look away from him. His eyes were dark, fathomless as he gazed at her, imploring her to meet him halfway, to look at him. A half smile formed on his lips as he watched her with that expression of his that accused her of lying. He knew her, understood how she felt.

"You must have been since you sought me out." His words were spoken with a bland indifference coupled with a mocking grin.

"I was just surprised. 'Twas a deer nothing more or less. No harm." Her words were staccato like spoken quickly as if her lungs still were robbed of air. Once more she pushed against him, to no avail. He would not let her go until he was ready, until...

"Could have been a man. Someone who wished you harm," he said softly. "I would not have liked that."

"You wish to do me harm." Even though she spoke the words accusingly she knew them to be false. He was experienced in the ways of sexual games between men and women, understood how to give and receive pleasure. She heard as much from her older brother when he warned her to stay away from the McKenna men. She just didn't understand what he wanted with her.

"Nay, I only wish to give you pleasure." His voice was whiskey smooth sending a telling shiver down her spine.

"I don't know what you're saying." She pointed down the trail where they were headed. "See, there is my home. You can leave now. You've seen me to my destination. I thank you to go now."

"Not until I'm ready and I know there is no one inside waiting for you."

His hands encircled her upper arms. He leaned forward as if he meant to kiss her yet he did not. Disturbed, irritated with herself for wanting just that, she trapped her lower lip beneath her teeth. She didn't desire him in her home. He would see how little she owned then he would press his case.

I want you.

Those three words reverberated in her head, her entire being crying out no, no, he could not have her as his mistress or anything else. *Stay strong.* She would have remained in London if being used by a man was her intent or even her destiny. Here, she had a purpose, a job to accomplish. That wasn't true. She could have never let her brother flee without help. His only crime was that he plead the Jacobite cause in the House of Lords. He was not a Jacobite, barely religious in any way. He had soundly fought for the English, fought for the Duke of Cumberland during the war where the Scots tried to set James on the throne. He had simply felt that two years after the last battle it was time to put the differences aside thereby living in peace with the Scots. Now all he yearned for was to find a means to help those who were persecuted.

"Shall we?" He beckoned toward her home.

She heard his voice, felt the whisper of his breath against her cheek, jerking her back to the present. "What?" She was shaking her head as he let her go. She had thought... What had she thought? That he was about to kiss her? Relief should be sweeping through her not this crazy disappointment.

"Go into your home. What did you think?" he asked as if he knew the answer before she could say.

"N-nothing. I wasn't thinking anything." At the blatant lie, she felt the flow of heat caress her cheeks.

He sent her a mocking all-knowing grin before nodding toward the door. "After you."

"Of course." She drew air into her lungs, felt the sting of the raindrops as she lifted her face away from him and his huge body no longer sheltered her. She stepped forward. At the door she paused to search his face. He was unrelenting, with only one purpose. She only wished she understood the reasons he singled her out for this torture.

Inside a small fire burned in the hearth. He gazed at the remains as well as the pot hanging over it. "Must have been a large fire you made this morning for it still to be burning. Whatever you've got cooking in that pot is most likely burned."

"I don't go to work until the afternoon, if you must know. The fire would hardly burn down to nothing."

"I will see that you work in the mornings instead. That way you won't have to walk home at night."

She laughed at him, "What? You don't intend to walk me home every night?"

"If the lass would let me stay every night in her bed, I'd be more than pleased to walk you home."

Not waiting or seeming to expect an answer, he helped her with her cloak, shaking the drops off outside the door before closing it and hanging the coat on its hook then he slipped out of his coat. Her stomach churned. The rabbit stew should have been inviting. She'd not eaten since this morning.

"Would you like some stew?" she queried, hoping for something to talk about before he pursued whatever plans he had for the evening.

"No, but don't let me stop you. Don't suppose you had a chance to eat," he said as he sat down, seemingly making himself comfortable.

"I couldn't eat a thing," she murmured, trying to look in any direction but at him. She needed to busy herself as well as her hands. "I'll clean it up and put in a container for tomorrow."

"It was nice of the laird to snare you a rabbit. Isn't something he usually does for a tenant."

She stopped surprised, as she tried to hide her emotions. She lowered her lashes. "It was," she lied.

By the look on his face, she guessed he knew. Yet his scowl told her he was thinking over something. "Why are you here?"

"I live here. Why are you here?" she shot back as she poured a glass of wine for herself and him. "I don't have tea."

"But you have wine."

She nodded. I drank the tea first. I've not been paid for my services so I can't purchase anything from the village. This is all I have," she paused for a moment. "and water of course."

"Wine is fine. Tomorrow I'll see your cupboards are stocked."

"Nay. Ye cannae."

"I can and I will."

"Why?"

"Because," he spoke slowly at first enunciating every word, "I plan on spending a great deal of time here—with you. I don't plan on being deprived of anything I want or like, beginning with you."

"I don't want you."

He rose, walking toward her, his smile firmly in place. "Let's see about that," he said softly.

"I would not like to see anything."

What an arrogant, self-centered bastard. He would do everything in his power to bend her to his will. She would do everything to prove he could not. Yet her hands were shaking, her breaths coming in tiny gulps as he pressed ever closer. His gaze was upon hers. His eyes turning to dark silver, heated to a fine sheen. He stood over her now.

"Did you realize that your fingers were moving on my chest just a few minutes ago when we stood outside in the freezing rain? You wanted me then. I'm gambling you still want me."

"They were not. You should leave now."

"In the freezing rain?"

One of his large hands wrapped around her neck, gently drawing her closer. Quickly, he undid the scarf holding her hair back. The length spilled around her shoulders. His fingers wound into her glorious hair. She felt the constant pressure at her nape. The other hand settled on her waist, stroking the curve of her hip. "No, I dinnae want this." Once more she lied.

"You will." Slowly his mouth descended, enclosing hers. He touched, stroked and nibbled across the width. His tongue moistened her lips, traced the crease between them His teeth tugged with the suggestion she open for him. Her mouth was wet and hot, swollen slightly where he caressed.

She resisted his subtle persuasion, refused to be drawn into the delicate coaxing, to the fire smoldering inside. He barely touched her and it seemed she could not draw a breath of air.

"Relax, sweetling. Give into what you are feeling. All will be as it should be." His hand stroked her back, up then down. Each pass of his hand drew her closer to the hard length of him. She felt the play of his muscles against her breasts as they began to swell and throb expectantly. She had never been kissed like this, never been unable to resist the sweet intoxication of a man's lips. The men she'd been with in London were nothing like this man.

Lilly clung to him simply because if she didn't she would crumple to the floor in a tiny ball of nothingness. Her fingers held on to his shoulders, her lips swelling under the fierce possessiveness of his mouth as he claimed her as his own. She stifled a silent whisper of expectations as he gently deepened the kiss, his tongue sweeping across her mouth finding entrance while he slowly parted her lips, his tongue delving inside, retreating then continuing the sensuous invasion. His hand stroked her back again and again then settled on her rear. As he pulled her between his legs, his hard arousal pressed against her.

"You want me," he whispered softly. "Admit it. Let me inside your sultry warmth. Melt in my arms. Let me dissolve in your fire."

Outwardly, she was still denying the feelings as well as the inferno he created within her. Inwardly, she was yearning for more, needing to feel the depth of his emotions as he enticed and lured her in ways she didn't understand to do his bidding. Refusing his insistent exploration was impossible as her hands rose higher, circling his neck. Her breasts pushed against his chest. It was everything she'd ever yearned for, to be kissed and treasured for who she was, not what she could bring to a marriage. Deep in her heart, she realized he wasn't treasuring her. He was using her for his personal needs. That fact made no difference at the moment.

This wasn't a marriage proposal, she reminded herself. If anything it was a proposal to become his mistress. She would not give in to his demands. She would resist anything more he might ask except the promise of his kisses.

She gave into his quest, opening her lips to his invasion. His tongue thrust inside then again as his lips molded to hers. He played her body as if she was created for him and him alone. Heat seared everywhere he touched then cooled when he withdrew. He nipped the corners of her mouth before stroking with his tongue and lips across her chin to her ear. He placed tiny kisses down her neck as her fingers wound into his hair in an unconscious attempt to bring him closer.

The tiny moan of pleasure rippling from her was nearly her undoing as she still tried to withhold some part of her from him. It was not to be simply because he would not allow her to hold anything back. When she tentatively touched his lips with her tongue, he sucked hers deep inside his mouth. With that simple gesture what she gave him was undeniable. His fingers clenched her body to his, tightening and squeezing her derrière until she could barely breathe, until she was pushing of her own volition against him as if she yearned to become one with him.

He pulled away as he looked down at her. Her head rested against his chest now. "Look at me," he said softly gifting her with a mocking smile that seemed to be meant to put her in her place. "Do you want me?"

She stiffened at the thought he so easily played her, toying with her. She willingly danced to the tune he set. This was just a prelude to the continuing games until he had her in his bed beneath him, her legs spread for him. She wouldn't be his plaything. Refusing his attentions in the future would not be easy. She knew she had to keep him from taking her innocence, from ruining her for a marriage.

And yet...

Lilly knew she had no prospects for a marriage, having knowingly left that part of her life behind her when she fled her betrothal and everything evil in London. The gossip surrounding her would put a stamp on her reputation that could never be erased. He would think less of her if he understood the extent of her lies and betrayals. Her father entered into the contract with good intentions.

She defied him.

Would do it again if faced with the same decision. She had no regrets. Perhaps becoming the mistress of a man such as Brady McKenna would not be so bad or humbling. Her fate could be worse. She might go through life without knowing the sweet pleasures a man could give a woman.

Brady McKenna was arrogant, a proud man who took what he wanted. He wanted her. Would that be so wrong?

"No," she told him. "No, I dinnae want you."

"Little liar, should I prove your statements are false?" he stroked her cheek, ran his fingertip along her collarbone.

She shivered in response, heat sweeping through her. Once again his mouth descended on hers, stroked and moved creating that same magical enchantment he crafted before. This time when his finger ran along her back he moved slightly. Now, his hand cupped her breast. Through the thin fabric of her gown he caressed the hard bud at the tip, torturing her with the burning need his hands and lips generated.

"If you didn't want me, you would tell me to stop," he whispered, his teeth closing over her ear, biting gently as his fingers caught her nipple, tugging. "I could take your breast into my mouth, suck it deeply and still you would not say no."

The last words angered her, bringing her back to the reality of the present. He knew what he was about. She allowed him to seduce her. "No." She pulled in a deep breath of air praying it would give her courage also. "Brady, stop. Please." Yet she heard the tone of her voice. It sounded as if she was pleading with him to continue not to cease.

He did stop then, sweeping her into his arms and striding with her to the small chair near the fireplace. Sitting down, he held her in his lap, continuing to caress her back the curve of her hip then back to her nape. It seemed to Lilly that he was trying to ease her not seduce.

"I want you, Lilly. I want you willing and begging me to kiss you, to touch you in places that only a man you care for will touch you. For now, perhaps we should sample that wine in our glasses and leave what comes next for another time."

"I won't ever beg," she told him lifting her chin, trying for an air of confidence she didn't feel. Bloody eyes but she wanted to beg him right now to kiss her again, to stroke her with his long fingers until... Determined, she would never give that kind of power over to him.

"No, Lilly, you probably will not. Perhaps beg is the wrong word to use with someone so proud." Still his fingers continued to move on her flesh, finding places that heated her as she continued to dissolve into him. Each stroke of his hand created a new fire where it burned only to turn cold when his fingers left. She tried to still the violent shivering of her body but could not.

"Please, I can take no more of this," she whispered.

"Only one thing will ease the desire you feel for me. I can do that. Ease the desire. All you need do is ask," he told her as he placed his lips on the thundering pulse at the base of her neck, lingering, touching, kissing.

"I cannae."

"Then we must wait until you want me more than you've wanted anything else your entire life. Will you want me, need me like that, Lilly?" His silken voice caressed her to her soul, made her hunger for things a lifetime of teachings had told her were wicked, sinful.

She should not, could not tell him yes.

Her brother would certainly disown her if she gave in to this man's plans. Her father had already done so. What did she care?

Her mind and body were weak.

"The rain has ceased." He swirled his tongue inside her ear.

She didn't understand his comment even now he was unfastening the front of her dress, moving the fabric aside so he could touch her, stroke her more intimately. "No!" She leapt to her feet, tugging the sides of her gown closed. "You must leave. As you said, the rain has stopped."

He smiled softly at her, his gaze moving from her breasts to the tips of her toes assessing just as he did when her hands were wrist deep in dough. "If that's what you want. A good-bye kiss first. One that will warm me through the night.

Before she could inhale again, she was in his arms, his lips touching upon hers once more, claiming them asserting himself.

Then, "I want you, Lilly. Don't ever forget that."

~ * ~

Brady left the cottage before he made the irrevocable mistake of taking Lily to bed before she would admit to wanting him. Pulling up the collar of his coat to shield his neck from the wind, he chuckled softly. She was passionate, a desirable woman as well. Her hair was as silken and soft as he thought it would be. She melted into him when he kissed her. Her breasts weren't overly large but they fit his hands to perfection. They were soft but firm, her flesh silken fire. With a little patience, he would win this game, coax her into giving all of herself to him.

Ah, but he could envision her naked in his arms.

About five minutes down the path leading to the castle, he doubled back, taking a more circuitous route to the cottage. When he mentioned the rabbit and his father's part in gifting her with the meat, she appeared genuinely surprised. The two sets of everything still bothered him. She was hiding something. Before he made love to her, he meant to discover some truths. Perhaps nothing was amiss and what she presented to him was true.

He didn't believe that.

Her home was in front of him now, the lights still shining in the main room. He hunkered down in the dark and waited. Minutes ticked by. The wind moaning around the trees surrounding him and still he waited. He shifted his weight from one foot to the other, groaning at the tightening of his muscles. Rain began to fall again. Tempted to shift, his thick cat fur would be a better barrier to the water than the coat he wore.

Perhaps he was wrong about Lilly. Maybe there wasn't a second person living with her. Quite possibly she wasn't hiding her true identity or her purpose. He heard the light tread of boots on the fallen twigs and leaves before he saw the shadow then the man. His breath caught in the back of his throat as he remained dead still. He watched. The man's fist rose to knock on the door.

"Douglas!" Lilly had thrown open the door then eagerly hurled herself into the man's arms.

"Deadly little liar," he murmured softly. His anger at her deception filled him. The question now was just who was Douglas and what did he mean to her? None of the crofters that he knew of went by that name. So, what would she tell him when he confronted her with the man?

The man kissed her on the forehead, a chaste kiss that sent his fists into tight balls. Jealousy was not an emotion he expected or ever experienced. On silent feet, he walked to one of the windows. Setting his back against the wall, he listened to the conversation between them.

"You cannot stay here any longer," Lilly told the man. "It's not safe and well you know it. You put me in danger as well as the clan. After all the McKenna has gone through to keep neutrality here, I cannot..."

"Hush now, Lilly. I would never do such a thing. Perhaps it is best I return and clear my name."

"Is such a thing possible?" she asked sounding breathless and out of sorts. When he snuck a peak at the couple, Douglas was holding her, her long slim body pressed against his. The man's hands were around her waist. A rage he'd never felt before simmered, waiting to explode.

"Perhaps not yet," he stroked her hair. "If I leave will you be safe here? This might be our last time."

"I ken it, Douglas."

I saw you with one of the sons."

"I'm sure I'll be safer than you," she told him softly. "Where will you go?"

"Farther into the highlands, north where fewer people live. I'll find a ship sailing for America. I've heard a man can live there, pursue his dreams." He kissed her again, a gentle kiss.

"I will think of you. I love you, Douglas. Where ever you go take care." She reached up, placing her palm on his cheek.

Brady's breath stopped as he digested her words, telling himself it didn't make any difference how she felt about that man. He still wanted her, the little harlot. When he first saw her, it made no difference to him how well used she was. Now he knew there had been at least one man in her life.

"If your father finds you?"

"I won't go back to London. I can't live that way nor can I marry that man father betrothed me to."

"You might not have a choice," Douglas said, smoothing her hair from her forehead. "The contract has been signed."

"You could stop it."

"Nay, not even if I could wed you myself, could this nightmare for us end. If you were to wed someone else, well, perhaps then."

"Who would want me, or want to take a chance? Lord Claymore is filled with revenge. He would kill anyone who took what he thinks is his."

"Lord Claymore cannot hold a pistol his hand shakes so bad."

"He can hire the finest assassins. You take care, little one. Don't let anyone sway you to do something you don't want to do. Don't let the McKenna—"

They both turned, searching the woods for the sound they heard. "Go," she said. "What if it's the English searching for you? For us?"

"It would be a random bit of luck on their foolish parts. No one of any position even realizes your mother was Scottish. That she lived here before she wed Lord Townsend."

Brady ducked down, moving silently behind a tree as he watched the couple from a greater distance, unwilling to give himself away.

"You will stop. Promise me you will stop."

"I cannot."

Other Books by Christine Young
Available at Rogue Phoenix Press

My Sweet Broc
Bad Boys Book One

He's a bad bad boy...

Broc Wallace is a fun-loving rake who never thought any beautiful woman could melt his heart. He lives life in the present enjoying the camaraderie of his friends and the pleasures of his mistress. When Bliss races into his life, he is ill prepared to deal with her secrets or give up the tenor of his life. When the truth is revealed, he finds himself unable to forgive and forget the betrayal.

... but she's sweet for him

Bliss MacTavish knows she's playing with fire when she refuses to tell this bad boy her name. He tempts her with sweet whispers of seduction knowing her innocent nature will be unable to refuse all he yearns to give her. Deciding to follow her heart, she finds the repercussions more than she bargains for when she gives herself to this bad boy.

Crazy for Cam
Bad Boys Book Two

He's a bad bad boy...

Lord Cam MacEwen, Viscount of Rosehill, tries his best to be proper and court the lady of his dreams in the acceptable way. The feat proves impossible when the lady in question uses every means at her disposal to tempt him. He fights his jealousy for another man as well as the need to make her his own, finally giving in to her irresistible passion.

... but she's crazy for him.

Chelsea MacTavish wants the bad boy she fell in love with and kissed just before her eighteenth birthday. With feminine wiles and irresistible allure, the sensuous lady plans to best Cam at his game of hearts and make him forget his need to court her properly.

Falling for Flynt
Bad Boys Book Three

He's a bad, bad boy...

Fascinated by Hope's loss of memory yet haunted by her sultry beauty, Flynt is irresistibly drawn to the stoic miss—and into her troubles with the sultan who wants her for himself. When he discovers she is the sister of his best friend, his pride keeps him from pursuing her and making her his.

... but she's falling for him.

Raised in a harem but now penniless, alone and without her memory, Hope must discover a way to remember all that she has lost. She finds a way to continue with her life as a servant in Flynt's home. The first sight of Flynt steals Hope's breath as well as her heart. Can she overcome her fears and give herself to the man she fell in love with.

Dancing With Donal
Bad Boys Book Four

He's a bad bad boy...

Once a bad boy always a bad boy, Donal Chamberlin's carefree ways come crashing down around him when he meets the ravishingly beautiful Daryl MacTavish, the innocent little sister of one of his best friends. He is determined to win her heart as he sets his sights on marriage and an heir. His past gets in the way of his quest when a woman he once loved threatens Daryl's life.

... but she's dancing with him.

Daryl has seen the control her sister's husbands hold over them. She yearns for a life where she makes decisions for herself. No man will have power over her. But no man kisses her the way Donal does. No man can make her forget all her goals leaving her helpless to give up her dreams. Yet Donal is determined to dance through all the barriers she thrust in front of him, pursuing her until she says yes.

Loving Leslie
Bad Boys Book Five

He's a bad bad boy...

Leslie Stewart, Duke of Southcliff is stoic, set in his ways, a spy who is used to having his life well ordered. He expects life to continue on in this perfectly conventional fashion. He assumes his bad boy status while keeping mamas and debutantes at arm's length. An heir is needed but Leslie has every intention of finding a woman who doesn't covet his wealth and tittle. He is irresistibly drawn to the headstrong young lady who becomes more beautiful as she develops into a woman.

...but she is loving him.

When Leslie kisses Lacie MacTavish, she knows even at the tender age of fifteen this is the man of her dreams. Forced to wait until she comes of age, Lacie withdraws into herself. Now she is eighteen and Leslie has returned from a mission for the British Government ready to claim her as his bride. She refuses him and he must find a way to seduce her and in the process create a burning passion within her, which she cannot deny.

Pleasing Arie
Bad Boys Book Six

He's a bad bad boy...

Arie Demir has never been denied anything in his life. He takes what he wants. What he undeniably yearns for is the beautiful redheaded spitfire he sees in a restaurant in Glasgow. At every turn, she confuses him by disputing his power over her. Alison refuses to accept the fact he owns her. While Arie tries desperately with patience and tenderness to drive her wild with new sensations, his scorching kisses ignite the fires of her very soul to make her understand he is all she will ever want.

...but is she pleasing him?

Alison Fletcher never expected to find herself kidnapped and sold to a whorehouse then bought by a Turkish sultan to become his slave. She vows to never surrender to the arrogant man who believes he owns her. She is stunned by the magnificently handsome man who awaits her compliance. Unexpectedly, she finds Arie the lesser of all the evils. The hidden depths of his mesmerizing dark brown eyes hold her into their power; his muscular embrace makes her weak with desire. She is his to do with as he wishes.

Graham's Wicked Kiss
Bad Boys Book Seven

He's a bad bad boy...

Graham Chamberlin is stunned to find three young boys dangling from the trees lining the drive to Runningmead Manner. On further inspection, he is astonished at their obsession to protect a young woman who has been brutalized by her pimp. The woman he discovers hiding in a third-floor attic room is gravely injured. He takes the silver haired stowaway under his wing. Clearly, Graham's new guest is a lady with many secrets. He is determined to unlock all the mysteries surrounding her.

...But she can't resist his wicked kiss.

The years since Ria left the convent where she was raised have been a nightmare. Her secrets are dangerous—as is the powerful man determined to find her. Handsome Graham Chamberlin is clearly a gentleman with secrets of his own, but staying with him could mean the difference between life and death for Ria. With each passing day, her handsome host turns Ria's convalescence into an increasingly sensual escape. Now her greatest challenge may be imagining anything less than a future in his arms.

Foolish for Piper

The pickpocket...

Piper has spent her life surviving the streets of St. Giles Parish in London, a den of iniquity and crime. Masquerading as a boy she escapes the whorehouses the young girls are sent to as they come of age. The day she encounters Brett MacLachlan begins the same as every other one. When she picks his pocket, she has no idea her life is going to change irreversibly.

... and the mark

Handsome aristocrat Brett MacLachlan has come to London for his amusement only to find his world turned upside down by a thief and her dog. From the moment he spots her, Brett knows there is something intrinsically wrong. In his arms, Piper discovers passion and joy. Yet secrets of her past haunt her, and a scar will tell the true tale as well as her identity.

Taylor's Destiny

She traveled to another time and place to change destiny...

Enjoying a day of sailing, Taylor Maxwell never expected after a suffering a concussion she would wake up in another century. A resilient independent woman in the twenty-first century, the blond beauty is ill prepared for life in the 1800s. Her first sight of the naval captain who rescues her makes her heart stop, giving her hope for her future.

His life is transformed by a woman who appears from nowhere...

Born to a life of ease, Reid Stewart defies the dictates of those born to aristocracy and chooses a life of adventure in the navy and as a spy for the crown. When he discovers a nearly naked woman on the bow of small sailing ship, his heart warms. His love for Taylor and his need to protect her from a man who pursues her might cost him his life as well as hers.

Caitlin's Duke

She played a fiddle in an Irish pub...

Caitlin O'Shea Is the most beautiful woman Roc Leighton has ever seen. With her blue violet eyes and long black hair she captivates him. In turn he mesmerizes Caitlin. Caught in the power of his gaze as he watches her, she is wise enough to know he desires her but will never give his heart to her. Caitlin has vowed to never be any man's mistress.

And fell in love with an English Lord...

Roc knows the first time he watches her play the fiddle and dance around the pub, she will be his next mistress. Despite her protest, he will find a way to convince her that her place is with him. While Caitlin's determination to keep her vows, fate takes a cruel turn and she is forced to seek refuge with Roc.

Catching Meara
Book One in the McKenna Clan Series

Meara Thorton was a feisty, world-class computer hacker—cornered by the FBI and shockingly given the chance to be their newly acquired technical analyst. Brilliant and intuitive, yet aching with the loss of everyone she has cared about, her restless heart led her to discover a love she fought and a world she didn't know could possibly exist.

Sweet Sexy Sadie
Book Two in the McKenna Clan Series

From the first time Sadie's eyes met those of Brody McKenna in the hot Sierra Madre Mountains, theirs was a potent attraction—not gentle, slow, and easy, but hot, hard, and all-consuming. The daughter of a dysfunctional family, Sadie had dreams no man could wrench from her with hot sex and an all-consuming passion. She'd challenge this alpha male with all the strength she possessed. But her red hair, fiery temperament, and indomitable spirit obsessed Brody... and he knew he had to find a way to show her he was more than he appeared and convince her to make a life with him.

Sweet Misbehavin'
Book Three in the McKenna Clan Series

Cast adrift after fleeing the home of Jokul, the ice demon, Atantsi, a firestarter, grew to womanhood as she moved through time to keep the demon from finding her. Though stubborn and courageous, she was ill prepared to use powers she had not been taught. Her first sight of the intoxicating Carr McKenna left her breathless, and her second encounter gave her hope for a future she never thought she had.

A playboy, a second son and a shifter, a man who thought his life would be carefree, Carr McKenna was shocked to discover the woman he'd paid as an escort is a firestarter who is running for her life. He is the leader of all the McKennas around the world and that he has multiple powers. His passion for Margo and the need to defend her might cost him his life as well as hers.

Sweet Talkin' Sugar
Book Four in the McKenna Clan Series

Lyonesse McKenna, was dreaming or was she? From the instant Lyn saw Deacon McClain across a black jack table in a crowed Las Vegas casino the unmistakable attraction sent Lyn's senses flying into overdrive. Her family of shapeshifters believed in soul mates. She'd always been skeptical yet she couldn't help but question the way her heart sped when he looked at her.

When Deacon appeared in Las Vegas he knew his first job was to save Lyn from a Sea Demon, but the next order of business was to convince her he would someday mean more to her than she'd ever expected. But her stubborn nature and unbendable spirit consumed Deacon... and he had to chase away all the demons real and imagined in order to win her heart.

Sweet Surrender
Book Five in the McKenna Clan Series

Ripped from her family at the top of Infinity Cliff, Kimi McKenna finds herself thrust somewhere into the future. Dark elements threaten to destroy the earth unless Kimi can work together with the white witch to stop the destruction. Confused by her mate's role in the conspiracy, she refuses to acknowledge the connection. But amidst raging fire and attacks on the people she is coming to hold dear, she allows Maska O'keefe into her heart.

Maska O'keefe has loved the beautiful shapeshifter for years. Unable to save her life years ago, he vows to watch over her as he is given a second chance to convince her that even though he is a witch and not a shifter, they are indeed soul mates. Kimi's divided loyalties between her family and the cause she is now a part of will determine their relationship. Only the part she plays as the messiah can bring this to a conclusion in the final battle.

Dakota's Bride
The first book in the Lakota/Pinkerton Series

When Emma St. John received her brother's letter imploring her to escape her stepfather's vengeful scheme and to trust Dakota Barringer with her life, she was willing to chance it. But the handsome, brooding riverboat owner Emma found in Natchez a danger of another kind. For Emma soon found herself surrendering to an unrelenting desire.

Raised by the Sioux when his parents were killed, Dakota had been betrayed once before by a white woman. He wasn't about to trust another, especially one claiming that her stepfather, a powerful U.S. senator, had framed her as a murderess. But he couldn't let Emma's intoxicating effect on him. Now Dakota would risk his very life to protect the innocent beauty who had seduced him with her tender love.

My Angel
The second book in the Lakota/Pinkerton Series

A BEAUTY IN BUCKSKINS
When her father decided to send her to a finishing school back East, Angela Chamberlain refused to be confined to stuffy drawing rooms. Instead, the daring spitfire who could shoot like a man and ride like the wind longed for a life of adventure and romance—and she knew exactly who could give it to her. Devil Blackmoor was a hired gun with a dangerous reputation. But Angela was willing to go to the ends of the earth to capture the handsome devil's heart.

A DEVIL IN DISGUISE
He'd come to America looking for excitement, but Devil Blackmoor got more than he bargained for when he encountered a beautiful rebel who answered his kisses with a wild innocence that touched his very soul. Yet standing between them were more obstacles than either ever dreamed. For Devil had strapped on a gun for the wrong man. And that made Angela his enemy. Now he'll have to choose between his duty and the woman he loves more than life.

The Locket
The third book in the Lakota/Pinkerton Series

The year is 1894. Seeking revenge for crimes against his family, Misha Petrovich follows a path that leads straight to Ariel Cameron's boarding house in Mist Harbor, Oregon. A family heirloom in Ariel's possession leads Misha to believe she is guilty. The locket has been handed down to the oldest girl in the Petrovich family for generations. Ariel is innocent of wrong doing, but her father is not. Misha is torn by his feelings for Ariel and his need for restitution against her father. Knowing that the relationship between them is fragile, Misha does everything in his power to protect Ariel's father. His efforts are to no avail when her father is shot. Ariel comes to realize Misha's steadfast courage and determination to protect her and her father despite what has happened to his family. Ariel's love and devotion heals Misha's heart.

The Talisman
The fourth book in the Lakota/Pinkerton Series

Running from a marriage that lasted one night, Dr. Moriah McKeown discovers the land she has settled on is coveted by determined and lawless men. Yet the proud young woman who once vowed never to abandon her home has second thoughts when her adopted children are threatened. Her only recourse is to enlist the aid of a dark, dangerous gun for hire.

Haunted by the past and a betrayal he will never forgive, Ian Civanovich uses his fast gun and his reckless courage to forget the faithlessness of a woman in his past. He will trust no female—nor will he rest until the threat hovering over Moriah McKeown is put to rest.

Forever His
The fifth book in the Lakota/Pinkerton Series

Struggling to come to terms with the part she played in Jacob St. John's death, Etta Barringer resigns from Pinkerton Agency and seeks peace and solace in a Rocky Mountain Cabin.

Jacob has vowed to discover the reason Etta has betrayed him, sold him out to his enemy and left him for dead.

Isolated in their cabin, they discover their love for each other and learn to trust. But the trust is shattered when Jacob learns she is married to his sworn enemy; the man who left him in the desert to die.

Allura's Secret
Twelve Dancing Princesses Book One

Allura McClellan is horrified by her father's decision to take out an ad in the Times awarding her to the man strong enough and smart enough to win her hand and uncover her secrets. She's an intelligent young woman who takes great delight in the freedom allotted to her by her father. She's well aware that marriage would effectively curtail the adventures she's shared with her sisters and cousins.

Hunter Gray is nothing like the other men who've arrived to vie for Allura's hand in marriage and everything that goes along with it. However, he is the first to refuse to concede defeat and pursue her despite her attempts to disguise her true appearance. It's her temperament that is of more concern to him than her looks. Hunter has worked all his life with the hope of someday owning his own land. Now that it looks like there's a very real possibility that everything he's ever wanted is within reach nothing is going to deter him – including Miss Allura's disagreeable disposition.

Amorica's Wager
Twelve Dancing Princesses Book Two

Amorica Hepburn was sent to London to find a husband. Finding a man was the last item on her agenda. With her two cousins, Amorica wagers she can dissuade her suitor before the others. Despite her efforts she discovers a chemistry that cannot be denied. Suddenly she is the arrogant man's wife, pledged to a marriage neither desire. But swept off to his ancestral home above the Dover cliffs and into his strong embrace, Amorica is soon possessed by a raging passion for the husband she had vowed to despise…

Damian Andrews couldn't afford to trust the emerald-eyed spitfire who happened upon his secret. Amorica's hatred of all men of his kind only inflames the war that rages between them. Still, he can not control the intense desire his stubborn bride inspires, or make her surrender to his will until he has conquered the headstrong beauty on the battlefield of love…

Ravyn's Marriage of Inconvenience
Twelve Dancing Princesses Book Three

A REGAL BEAUTY
When the duchess decides to wed her to a wastrel and a fop, Ravyn Grahm takes matters into her own hands and declares her engagement to another man. Instead of fessing up and telling her great aunt what she has done, she goes through with the pretense. Ariec Lakeland is the bastard son of an earl and has a dangerous reputation. But Ravyn is willing to do most anything to keep the duchess from discovering the lie.

A DEVIL-MAY-CARE SMUGGLER
He'd bought land in America, looking to put down roots and end his life of adventure, but Ariec Lakeland got more than he bargained for when he encountered a beautiful heiress who made a promise she didn't want to keep. But the promise could not be undone and standing between them were more obstacles than either ever dreamed. Ariec had made plans to spend the rest of his life in America and that was at odds with Ravyn's plan of living in England and running her father's estate. Now, he'll have to choose between his dreams and the woman he loves more than life.

Christel's Sunrise
Twelve Dancing Princesses Book Four

He Made Her An Offer...
Life has thrown Christel McClellan some experiences that could

have devastated a less determined woman. Beautiful, self-assured and fiercely independent, she is trying to forget the loss of her stillborn child. But is the child alive?

She Couldn't Deny...
Life is carefree for Ryder MacLaren who loves to see what is on the other side of the sunrise. Laird of Clan MacLaren, he is wealthy, handsome and happily unencumbered... until stunning Christel McClellan enters his life. When he hears her story, he believes the child she thought dead has been sold to a wealthy buyer.

Storm's Passion
Twelve Dancing Princesses Book Five

SHE MADE A PROPOSAL...
Life strikes Storm Graham a shattering blow when she learns her father has bartered her to a man she detests. Storm is beautiful, self–assured and fiercely independent, and refuses to be a pawn in her father's schemes, yet she can find no way out of this bargain made in hell. Going on the offensive she asks the wealthiest man on the eastern coast of England to marry her, never believing she might fall in love.

HE TRIED TO REFUSE...
For Hadden Johnston life has provided everything he ever wanted, including a sanctuary for homeless children. He is wealthy, handsome and happily unencumbered... until stunning Storm Graham marches into his life and proposes a marriage of convenience. Yet this type of marriage to a woman who inflames his senses is far from acceptable. If he's going to be tied down, he will move heaven and earth to have this woman warming his bed.

Gotta Have Fayth
Twelve Dancing Princesses Book Six

A regal beauty with raven hair and piercing blue eyes, Fayth Graham is unwilling to parade herself in front of the wealthy Lords of England during the season. Seeking a means to dissuade any man wishing to wed her, she seeks a way to ruin herself for marriage. When she unexpectedly meets a man with sparkling gray eyes and an infectious grin, she decides this is the man who will keep her from agreeing to obey.

He returned from six months at sea, looking for a few nights of pleasure with a willing lass, but Jarret Kinsley got more than he bargained for when he met a beautiful debutant who responded to his kisses with a wild innocence that touched his heart. Yet the obstacles looming between them might rip them apart. Both had vowed never to marry, so when consequences of their dalliances got in the way, Jarret would have to choose between the life he's always desired and the woman he loves more than life.

Ella's Pleasure
Twelve Dancing Princesses Book Seven

A WHISPER OF PLEASURE
Ella Hepburn was an auburn haired debutant from the harsh Scottish coastline—a wild innocent to be seduced and tamed. A spirited beauty, she captivated Drake Montgomerie's jaded heart—while succumbing to the smoldering desire she felt for her unyielding suitor.

A WHISPER OF DANGER
In Drake Montgomerie's glittering world of money and privilege, young Ella discovered passion and desire could overcome everything she'd been taught to resist—entangling Drake, the heir apparent, in a lethal coil of aristocratic family intrigue. But grave peril would only nurse the sparks of a love that knew no limits and a magnificent ecstasy that would not be denied.

Eveleen's Seduction
Twelve Dancing Princesses Book Eight

A WHISPER OF SEDUCTION

A brutal attack on Eveleen Hepburn's cherished island off the Scottish coastline leaves her shattered and bewildered. Learning a man she once trusted can kill as easily as he can breathe even though the deed saves her life, creates questions that need answers. An innocent beauty, she enchants Logan Maxwell's cynical heart—giving in to the raging passion she feels for her mysterious suitor.

A WHISPER OF INTRIGUE

In Logan's Maxwell's world of espionage and privilege, young Eveleen discovers truths about herself she never expected, and a need for passion and love can overcome all her fears if she learns to accept certain truths. She finds herself entangled in a lethal battle for land that was once owned by French nobility, taken from them during the revolution and sold to Maxwell. But grave peril would unleash the flames of love that simmers, creating a magical union that cannot be refuted.

Tavia's Deception
Twelve Dancing Princesses Book Nine

WHISPERS OF DECEPTION

When her father decides to send her to London for her season, Tavia Hepburn resolves to see the world instead. The raven haired beauty decides to disguise herself as a lad and find employment on a ship bound for Barcelona as a cabin boy. But she never bargains on finding passion and love to a red haired sea captain who rescues her from certain death.

WHISPERS OF MURDER

For James Macmurra, the world is black and white until he meets a young debutante, who turns his world upside down. He's unable to deny Tavia's intoxicating effect on him. In a match tense with obstacles, unwillingness to divulge secrets, and unforeseen peril, irresistible desire and passion grows into undeniable love. James would risk his life to shelter and protect the innocent debutante who seduces him with her sweet love.

Larena's Fascination
Twelve Dancing Princesses Book Ten

WHISPERS OF FASCINATION

Fiery, free spirited Larena Graham never wanted to marry a duke. She is thrilled to be in love with the fourth son of an aristocrat, Gavin Broon. But when it seems Gavin ignores her, she set her sights on politics and bettering human life. Unsuspecting intrigue and a plot against her, she continues her dangerous plans despite Gavin's wishes.

WHISPERS OF TRUST

Gavin has every intention of properly courting the beautiful Larena until he must leave the city in order to put his affairs in order. Returning to London, he finds the woman he means to make his own is embroiled in political protests that could lead to a prison ship. Larena must learn to trust the handsome Scotsman whose most pressing mission is to protect her and keep her from harm.

Tira's Education
Twelve Dancing Princesses Book Eleven

WHISPERS OF EDUCATION

Learning how to build ships is Tira Hepburn's only dream until she meets Jamie Lundin and her world is turned upside down. With her raven black hair and vivid green eyes, she tempts Jamie and pushes him to defy his vows. She never bargains on finding an irrevocable love and a passion to a man who cannot fulfill her dreams despite his burning desire for her.

WHISPERS OF A BARGAIN

Arrogant and self-assured Jamie is brought up short when Tira captures his heart. All his carefully made plans are put to the test when he decides to teach her the art of ship building if she will spend a week with him alone on his ship. He is unable to deny Tira's intoxicating effect on him. When Tira leaves him behind unwilling to live with him without the benefit of marriage, he races after her. Jamie will risk everything to shelter and protect the innocent debutante who seduces him with her sweet love.

Aidan's Love
Twelve Dancing Princesses Book Twelve

Whispers of Love
Aidan McLellan has loved since she first set eyes on him as a young girl. Spontaneous, wild and eager to grow up, Aidan haunts his waking thoughts day and night, insinuating herself into his life. With her fiery red hair and sparkling sapphire eyes, she seizes Blade's heart even while he tries to resist the innocent child until she becomes a woman.

Whispers of Courage
Blade has waited what seems a lifetime to claim the woman who captures his heart as a little girl. Claiming his inheritance before his younger brother takes what is rightfully his, Blade must convince Aidan of his sincerity after years of avoidance and wed her before his father dies so he can return home, securing his rightful place. Everything is put to the test when his life as well as Aidan's is threatened by the man who once called him brother.

Twelve Days to Love

When Archer Steele shows up at Calanthe Durand's failing plantation with an alligator over his shoulder, Cali thinks she's never seen a more handsome man. During the war she had to defend herself and her servants from both union and confederate soldiers. Independent and self-sufficient, she vows to never marry.

But Archer Steele has different ideas. The first time Archer sees Cali in town, he feels an instant attraction. He decides he will do everything and anything to convince the beautiful Miss Durand he is worthy of her love. During the weeks leading up to Christmas, he gives her twelve gifts in hopes she will fall in love with him. Yet they are faced with challenges they must overcome before Cali can commit to a marriage.

Door to Heaven

Jessica Lawrence is the stepdaughter of a woman born in the twentieth century transported back in time to the year 1868. An acclaimed suffragette, she raises Jessica to believe in the equality of women. Jess Law believes everything she was taught, and when the time is right she becomes a private investigator. Courageous and impetuous, Jess finds danger in her quest to save all women from white slavery. Her passionate mission results in a wedding to Roc Newman, a man she knows can steal her heart...

Roc can't trust the sapphire-eyed spitfire who invades his home in search of secret papers and knocks him flat with her karate moves. Jessica's refusal to obey his wishes serves to inflame the war between them. Still, he cannot control the intense desire his reluctant bride inspires, or make her surrender her independence, until he has conquered the headstrong beauty on the battlefield of love...

Rebel Heart

HER REBEL SPIRIT DEFIED HIS OUTSIDERS SOUL... She was velvet and silk, eyes the color of a summer storm and amber hair. Victoria DeMontville, because of a promise and a codicil to her father's will, was forced to marry one man to protect her from another. She hated Cameron Savage with a fierce passion. But to hold on to her genetic research and find a cure for the deadly Signe virus, she must pretend to love the enemy at her door, come with weapons of fire to melt her icy heart...

HIS OUTSIDERS TOUCH IGNITED RAGING PASSIONS...
He wore a mask, disguised as the Phantom, a true legend come to life. Even as war and debate over new genetic research engulfed them all, he would find his greatest adversary in the beauty who'd branded him an outsider and barbarian, the woman he was born to possess, his soul mate.

Safari Moon

Solo St. John, a wildlife photographer, is preparing for a trip to Alaska. Suddenly, Solo finds women of all sorts invading his privacy, his home and his office, all cooing nonsense words and blatantly throwing themselves at him. Solo doesn't know why, and he has no idea how to rid himself of the persistent women. He finally decides to beg a favor of his best buddy Nyssa Harrington.

In love with Solo for the past ten years and knowing he doesn't return her feelings Nyssa doesn't want to talk to Solo. She knows if she accepts his phone call, she will not be able to resist the temptation to hope again.

Straight to Heaven

Running from demons, Alexandra McMurdie stumbles into Forbidden Ground where up is down and elements of nature are contested. Though a strong independent woman in the twenty-first century' she is unprepared for life in the 1800s. Her first site of the formidable James Lawrence makes her heart skip a beat, giving her cause to reconsider her desperate need to find a way home.

Born with a silver spoon, James' life was torn apart during the War Between the States. Moving west he vows to put the life he once knew in the past. When he discovers a half-frozen woman near Gold Hill, his heart begins to thaw. His love for Alexandra and his need to keep her from a man who has pursued her through time might cost him his life as well as hers.

A Valentine's Anthology

The Lending Library-a fantasy by Christie L. Kraemer
Faeries try to fit into the human world when the forest where they make their home is destroyed by a mysterious enemy.

Chasing Rainbows-a contemporary romance by Genene Valleau
An eccentric aunt, an inventive uncle, a mother who wears poodle skirts, and a brother who wears pearls provide a hilarious backdrop for the courtship of a young woman who yearns for a "normal" family.

The Gift-an historical romance by Christine Young
A man and a woman on opposite sides of the Civil War get a second chance at love after one final battle returns soldiers to their war-torn homes to rebuild their lives.

A St. Patrick's Day Tale
Christine Young, C. L. Kraemer, Genene Valleau

Tumble through time…

…to Ireland in 1817, when tensions are high between Protestants and Catholics and fae people guide the fate of villagers. A lovely Catholic lass stumbles upon the weakly ritual fisticuffing between Irish lads. She falls into the lap of a handsome young Protestant. Family ties, grudges, and two conniving faeries threaten their budding love. But the faeries outsmart themselves when they hijack a time machine that has mysteriously appeared in their forest and are whisked to…

…Eugene, Oregon in the 20th century, amid a property feud between the local faeries and night elves. The conniving faeries from Olde Ireland try to stir up more mischief. However, a warrior gnome convinces the magic folk to control their own destiny, and forces the intruding faeries to take refuge in the time machine again, spinning their way toward…

…A modern day castle in western Oregon. An eccentric inventor is determined to reclaim his wayward time machine and save his beloved wife from her latest misadventure. If only they can travel safely past the black hole…

a May Day Anthology
Christine Young, C. L. Kraemer, Rosemary Indra, Genene Valleau

Highland Miracle — Christine Young
HURTLED THROUGH TIME, Sean Michael Sterling, landed in the midst of a May Day celebration he didn't understand, assuming the role of Laird Sterling.

ILLIGITAMATE CHILD OF NOBILITY, Reagan Douglas searches for a way out of her half brother's house.

Defying the Odds — C.L. Kraemer
The night elves on the hill aren't happy without their magic. They concoct a plan to punish those who were involved in the act that rendered them almost human. Meanwhile, Uther, the rogue night elf, has returned to woo the Librarian to be his eternal mate.

Love in Bloom — Rosemary Indra
When childhood friends reunite it takes two fairies and a matchmaking daughter to help them admit their true love for each other.

No More Poodle Skirts — Genie Gabriel
After drifting for years in the innocent age of the 1950s, a woman struggles to join today's world by finding a career and a new love, with some help from her zany family.

Once Upon a Christmas Moon
Christine Young, C. L. Kraemer, Genene Valleau

TWELVE DAYS TO LOVE
When Archer Steele shows up at Calanthe Durand's failing plantation with an alligator over his shoulder, Cali thinks she's never seen

a more handsome man. During the war she had to defend herself and her servants from both union and confederate soldiers. Independent and self-sufficient, she vows to never marry. But Archer Steele has different ideas. The first time Archer sees Cali in town, he feels an instant attraction. He decides he will do everything and anything to convince the beautiful Miss Durand he is worthy of her love. During the weeks leading up to Christmas, he gives her twelve gifts in hopes she will fall in love with him.

BOOTS AND BLADES

An ancient evil from the old country has arrived in the high desert of Oregon. Gnome children are vanishing then re-appearing, showing various stages of traumatization. Tiamoon, warrior gnome, will put her skills to use alongside Killian, a handsome warrior, also in need of a cause.

CHRISTMAS PAWSIBILITIES

With their world destroyed and their space ship malfunctioning, the dogizens of Planet Canid have little choice but to crash land on Earth. They face tortuous experiments at the hands of the Geeks in Green... or they can trust an eccentric inventor and his zany family to deliver the Canine Queen's puppies and help them celebrate new lives.